Come In from the Cold

Marsha Qualey

Houghton Mifflin Company
Boston 1994

Library of Congress Cataloging-in-Publication Data

Qualey, Marsha.
   Come in from the cold / Marsha Qualey.
      p.   cm.
   Summary: The Vietnam War protest movement brings together two Minnesota teenagers.
   ISBN 0-395-68986-4
   1. Vietnamese Conflict, 1961–1975—Protest movements—Juvenile fiction. [1. Vietnamese Conflict, 1961–1975—Protest movements—Fiction. 2. Minnesota—Fiction.]   I. Title.
PZ7.Q17Co   1994   93-42064
[Fic]—dc20   CIP
                          AC

Printed in the United States of America
BP   10   9   8   7   6   5   4   3   2   1

We are stardust, we are golden, and we've got to get ourselves back to the garden.

—*Joni Mitchell, 1969*

All we ever wanted was to come in from the cold.

—*Joni Mitchell, 1991*

• *Part I* •

American Casualties, 1969

· 1 ·

Everybody was talking about Steve's spectacular tumble. While water-skiing that afternoon he had hit a wave just exactly wrong, shot up, and flipped over backward. His ski slipped off and slammed down on his back, the rudder slicing a seven-inch gash.

Keller and some other boys had been in the boat, and they described the accident again and again as people arrived at the party. Each time a boat approached the shore it would ease into a spot next to the last one beached, and the kids would get out and immediately run to the tightly clustered crowd by the bonfire.

"Take a look at Steve's back," they'd hear. Then Keller or one of the other boys would get another chance to tell their tale. The story got better as the crowd got bigger, and the response grew richer as the beer and pot circulated faster. Steve finally tired of displaying the bandage that was taped to his tanned back. He put on a shirt, found a beer, sat by the fire, and let his girlfriend nurse the wound with her fingertips and soft kisses.

That was everyone's cue to get a drink or to pair off and slip into the dark areas of the beach beyond the

3

reach of the bonfire. Keller had brought a portable tape player, and he turned it on. The reels rolled sedately while a frenzy of guitar and drum music screamed out of the speakers. A small group of people started dancing by the fire, forming a circle of hand-clapping, gyrating figures of shadow and light.

Someone produced a Frisbee, and a few of the boys tossed it across the bonfire, aiming each toss lower into the flames until the disc finally slammed into a log, knocking it out of the burning circle. Sparks flew and smoke billowed, forcing the dancers and the people seated by the fire to scuttle back. A loud protest compelled the boys to put away their toy. They then got cans of beer from the cooler and tossed those until one slipped out of someone's hand, hit a rock, and popped open. Beer spewed out and splashed over several girls who had gathered to watch the can-tossing. They complained about the mess. "You ruined my suit," one of them said, and all the girls looked with dismay at their swimsuits. They were wearing bikinis. One of the boys stepped up to one of the girls and apologized. "It will wash off," he said, "if we go swimming." He grabbed her hand, and they ran into the lake. The other bikinis followed, accompanied by some of the boys. Pretty soon the boys were tossing one of the girls, taking hold of her arms and legs and heaving her high overhead. She splashed down with a squeal. The other bikinis lined up to take turns.

Maud Dougherty emptied her soda into a depression in the sand. The liquid pooled for a moment, then was sucked away. Pot smoke drifted across her space and she exhaled forcibly, holding still for a moment when her lungs reached empty. She relaxed and let air rush back in. She decided she was prudish (Keller's word), but there had never before been pot at the beach parties. She knew that if the game warden on his daytime patrol found any roaches among the litter, the parties — just barely tolerated now because of all the underage drinking — would be closed down for good.

Maud shook her can, rattling the tab she had dropped inside to avoid losing in the sand. Everybody was careful about dropped tabs; sliced feet hampered water-skiing. She rose and moved around the party site, picking up empty snack bags and beverage cans and searching for roaches and cigarette butts. She supposed she shouldn't care about the mess, shouldn't care if all these tan, lithe, loud, and happy people had their summer fun curtailed because of cut feet or the warden's displeasure. She *didn't* care. But she hated a mess.

The wind had increased, blowing the sky clear of clouds, and now moonlight illuminated the beach and water. Maud looked at the perfect white circle. Hard to imagine that only last week men had actually walked on the moon. Played golf, danced around, acted like boys at a beach party. And they had left a mess there, too.

As she deposited the trash in a rusty garbage barrel, someone moved behind her. Maud turned and nodded to an unfamiliar boy. He smiled, then lifted a beer can to his mouth and took a long drink. She watched his Adam's apple bounce with each gulp.

Maud raised her eyebrows. It was an impressive display of consumption. She wondered if he meant it as some sort of mating call, like ruffling bright plumage. When he finished he dropped the can to the ground and flattened it with his bare foot.

"Is that smart?" said Maud. "You could get a nasty cut."

"Naw," he said. "Naw." He smiled and stepped closer to her. "So, um, are you, um, with a guy?"

One syllable noises. She could do that, too. "Um. No."

"Great. Far out." Even closer.

Maud chewed on her lip. One touch, and there'd be a knee in his nuts.

"So, like, should we . . ." He tipped his head toward the woods.

Do what? Discuss modern German literature or French cinema? Examine fungi?

Maud toed the sand. What had she expected, anyway? She'd known for years that the parties were little more than mating dances. This guy was so hopeful; she could at least be friendly. Maud put her hand on his shoulder. His eyes widened with hope. She rubbed. His legs stiffened and he stood straighter. "Do you know what I really like to do when I feel wild?" she whispered. His hand started stroking his bare chest.

"Tell me," he croaked. "Tell me." *Too good to be true!* his eyes screamed. *I'm gonna get laid!*

6

Maud snapped her body ramrod-straight, mussed her hair, then held out her arms with the hands cupped upward and the fingers spread open. "Imitate vegetables. Broccoli."

He stepped back, and his eyes sent a new signal: *Mad girl, mad girl!* He forced a smile. "Um, I guess I'll go get a beer."

"People loved it in theater class," Maud called after him. They had, too. She had been the hit of improv day.

The boy didn't return from the cooler. Maud felt a twinge of sympathy for him. After all, finding someone for an evening of at least kissing and groping was the point of the parties. She shouldn't have come if she wasn't going to play.

Maud looked out at the happy group in the water and saw that Keller had joined them. She watched as he helped one of the bikinis adjust a strap loosened by a hard landing.

"There goes my ride home," she said softly as she watched them kiss. Keller's family owned the cabin next to her own, and he had convinced her to come to the party.

Maud bent over to pick up more beer cans, and when she straightened she was facing a girl. Maud smiled. "Hello."

The girl shook her beer furiously and then aimed it at Maud's face as she ripped off the tab. Maud's eyes were caught open by the blast, and the stinging pain made her wheel around and drop her handful of trash.

"What are you doing?" she cried as she wiped her

face. People rose from their seats by the fire or walked toward them from the water, and a few couples popped out from the shadows. The dancers halted, but the music continued, the Stones wailing on. Maud turned and glared at the girl. "Who are you?"

The girl's long blond hair was pulled into a tight tail that stretched her face back an extra inch. She was tall and thin, but had large breasts that were not entirely covered by a loose tank top.

Maud pushed her hands into the pouch of her hooded sweatshirt. Beer ran off her nose and dropped into a nostril. "Who are you?" she repeated.

"My brother . . ." The girl's chest heaved as she found air for the words. Maud looked down at her own front, nearly a flat plane to her feet. "My brother died last March."

Maud wrinkled her brow. "I'm sorry."

"In Vietnam. He was a corporal, and he got shot. He was nineteen."

Maud now knew what was happening and what would come next. She looked across the lake and calculated the distance to her cabin. Maybe a mile. She saw some scattered yellow lights and wondered which was hers. She'd left a light on in the kitchen.

"Steve said that woman was your sister."

"What woman?"

"The one the FBI wants. The one who poured paint over the president's car. The one who shot two policemen in Chicago. The one who let rats loose in the convention."

Maud couldn't restrain a smile. She had always thought the mice — they were really only mice — were a good trick. She looked at the angry girl. "She didn't shoot anyone. She only bought the guns."

The girl slapped her. Maud stepped forward, ready to strike, but someone restrained her. "She's flipped out," Keller whispered. His hand stroked Maud's arm. "Don't do anything."

The girl screamed. "Your *sister* should be dead, not my brother. All he did was go fight so people could be free. Someone should shoot your sister!" People backed away from her.

Maud turned to Keller. "Take me home?"

"You bet."

A girl behind him protested. Keller turned and gave the girl a quick kiss. "Another night."

Maud had always hated the big powerboats that were becoming more popular on the lake. Tonight, however, she appreciated the speed with which Keller's took her from the party. She closed her eyes and tipped her head back over the edge of the seat. This was so different from being in a canoe, where the orderly dip and pull, dip and pull would send the small craft along slowly, carefully, deliberately. This boat roared and rushed over the waves, bouncing as it hit the crests of the high ones. A loud, wild ride at the edge of chaos. Was anyone in control?

Maud opened her eyes and turned to Keller. He was standing behind the steering wheel and looking through the dark for a landing clue that would let him

9

find the right dock along a mile of dark forest. He slowed the boat down, and the shift in noise level was welcome.

"Sorry about the bikini," Maud said.

"What?"

"The girl. It looked like you had a good night going and I ruined it."

"Maybe not so good. She was kind of dumb."

"How would you know? You were doing more tossing than talking."

Maud put her feet up on the side of the boat. Water spray wet the soles of her sandals. "Who was she?"

"Just a girl."

"No, now I mean the one with the dead brother."

"Steve's dad's boss's daughter. Her family's here for a week. Damn, I thought I left the dock lights on." Just as he spoke, a string of blue lights began flashing on shore. Keller's father had rigged them early in the summer as a way to identify the dock in the night. "Once again, Mom's waiting and worrying." He turned the boat slightly and headed home.

While Keller secured the boat in its hoist, Maud lay on the dock and splashed lake water on her face and hair to rinse off the odor of beer. When she finished and sat up, Keller squatted next to her. "Do you want to go into town for some food?"

She shook her head.

"Come in and play cards? My dad would love to win back that five dollars from you."

"I don't feel like it."

"Then why don't we lie down and make out like the old days?"

"Dream on, Keller." She pulled him down, and they sat with feet skimming a fraction of an inch above the water.

The silence was comfortable and familiar. Maud didn't know any other girl her age who was so friendly with the first boy she'd ever kissed. That had happened three years before when they were fourteen, the summer Maud's mother died and her sister Lucy dropped out of college and went to Europe to roam around. Maud had come down to the dock one rainy afternoon. She'd covered herself with a big green poncho large enough to be a tent and sat and watched the rain. Keller had joined her, sitting silently under his own green poncho. They sat for nearly an hour, two green bumps against a field of gray rain and lake water. When Keller's mother called him in for dinner, they rose and faced each other. Keller stepped closer, then kissed her.

"Nice," she'd responded. And he did it again.

After two weeks of good-night kisses and some slightly more serious necking at beach parties or while lying on the dock at night, she had pushed him away one evening when he held her outside her cabin door. She looked from him to the porch light that was plastered with bug bodies. "I'm not sure why," she said, "but I don't want to anymore."

"Yeah, that's okay. It's kind of weird making out with someone who used to sleep over in the top bunk."

11

"Exactly." They'd gone to his cabin then to play cards with his sisters.

They remained good friends. The previous fall, Maud's sister had received all sorts of publicity for the protests at the political conventions and she had gone underground with companions to avoid arrest and police questioning about the guns she'd bought and who had used them to kill two Secret Service agents. Later, Maud had received a postcard from Keller. All he had written was, "The mice were great. K."

A boat passing in the distance sent a small wave rolling toward them. It washed over their feet, and a chill rushed through Maud. Even in August the lake water wasn't warm.

She drew up her knees and hugged them. "For all we know she's dead."

"You would have heard something. She's alive. And giving people hell, too. God, the way she used to bitch at me about wearing a life jacket when I was skiing. She was such a mother about boat rules."

"You were so bad about breaking them. Oh, Keller, I wish she'd write or something. A call. Just two words: *I'm okay.* Dad never says much, but I can tell he's going crazy. He probably doesn't know whether he's mad as hell at her or worried sick."

"Maud, if she did try to reach you the FBI would swoop down. She has to know they've got you covered."

"Or maybe she just doesn't care. I wonder if she's thought even once about how much I'd miss her. Once. Did that matter to her?"

"I'm sure it did."

"But not enough." Another boat crossing the water caught their attention. Visible only as an outline of lights suspended in the dark, it drifted across the black horizon. As they watched and listened to the boat's slow progress, Maud's thoughts drifted and she recalled a phone call with Lucy before her round of political protests. The three-way call — Lucy in Miami, Maud in the kitchen, their father in his study — had dissolved into a pleading and shouting match.

"Of course I love you," Lucy had finally roared. "But, no, I don't care about the family. The family is just another sick part of the diseased bourgeois social structure, Father. The whole damn structure is twisted and knotted up. It's turned in on itself, and something has to happen to break it loose and free."

I don't care. She had said that. Maud rose from the dock. "I'm tired."

"Are you sure you don't want to sleep on our porch? Mom worries about you staying alone."

Maud smiled. "I'm not welcome in the top bunk anymore?"

"Fine with me, but the old folks would have a fit."

"I'm okay at home, Keller. I like it alone."

"Mom's going to town tomorrow. Need anything?"

"I have a car, remember? I'm fine, Keller. Anyway, I think I'll paddle to Barnum Lake and camp for a couple of days."

Keller shook his head. "You shouldn't go by yourself."

"Don't nag."

Keller rose and kissed her on the cheek. "If you aren't back by supper on Thursday I'll come get you."

"Thanks, Mommy."

Maud had been alone at the family cabin since June. The day school got out she had packed a duffel bag with clothing and two shopping bags with food and headed north out of Minneapolis in her car. It was her own car, bought with her own money the day she got her driver's license. Her father had disapproved but wouldn't interfere. "It's your money," he said. "Your mother left it to you, and it's yours to spend."

And Lucy's was hers to spend — his obvious, unspoken thought. To spend on guns, and blood-red paint, and mice, and poorly written, vitriolic underground papers that decried the conditions of the world. Compared to those weapons of revolution, a car seemed like a harmless purchase.

It had been a solitary two months, but not lonely. Keller's family and other friends were watchful, Maud's father called often, and she kept busy.

First she painted the trim on the cabin a dark brown, covering the whimsical pink her mother and Lucy had painted years before. She patched holes in the screens, learned to unplug a toilet, and befriended the staff of the hardware store in town. She'd made progress on a quilt for her father, identified five new wildflowers, and taught herself to fillet a fish. And every night she'd gone to bed hoping that that night would be the one her sister came home.

Even in the coolest weather, or through the strongest storm blowing out of the northwest, Maud slept with her window open at least a crack. She imagined that's how she would know Lucy had returned — a soft scratch on the screen, a terse order to meet somewhere in the woods. Maud knew it was why her father approved of her staying alone in the cabin until he was done teaching summer session at his college in St. Paul. If Lucy wanted to see them, it would only be possible here.

But that night, again, Maud heard nothing meant for her in the soft symphony of forest noise.

· 2 ·

Maud shivered in the early morning air. Six A.M., and there was no hint of the August heat that would develop in a few hours. She zipped up her sweatshirt and stepped carefully into the canoe. She pushed off from the dock, dipped her paddle, and the canoe moved forward. She headed toward the sunrise, smoothly lowering and lifting her paddle — a solitary figure in motion on the expanse of glassy green water.

Barnum Lake was five miles northeast of Maud's lake. To reach it she'd have to portage twice and paddle through several lakes and a small creek that was sometimes overgrown with wild rice and lily pads. Then there was a final rocky portage.

Recent rains had made the creek full and free-flowing, but had eroded the steep hills on the last portage. When she reached this last stretch, the early morning cool was long gone and she sweated through it, swatting angrily at the mosquitoes that swarmed around her face under the canoe as she carried it on her shoulders. She walked as quickly as she could with a heavy pack on her back and the canoe balanced on her shoulder yoke.

"I'd like to see a bikini do this!" she shouted in the echo chamber under the canoe.

The final twenty yards of the portage were a mud-slicked slide downhill. Maud dug the heels of her leather boots into each step, but she couldn't stop from gaining speed and she was running by the time she reached the shore. She ran straight into the water, lost her balance, and fell. The canoe rolled off and landed right-side-up. The pack slipped off her shoulders and sank.

"Hey," she said to the air, "I meant to do it that way." She dunked her head in the cool water to relieve the stinging of bug bites.

Maud loaded the canoe and set off toward the campsite. The canoe was lightweight and easy for one person to guide and propel, especially on a small lake like Barnum, where the high, forested hills shielded the water from wind.

The lake was narrow and about the length of two football fields. There was a small public landing at the end of a rutted, gravel township road, but she had never seen any fishermen. There were no cabins and no public campsites. Years ago, Lucy had noticed the small lake on a map and decided to explore. She went alone the first time and came back to announce she'd found paradise, right in Minnesota. Maud went with her often after that. One time they'd taken Keller and their fathers, but only one time.

Maud stopped paddling and stared at the shoreline, where there was a small patch of sand, the only sandy spot on the lake. A slight gust of wind blew back branches, and she saw a flash of red, the very same red as her sister's favorite camping shirt. "Lucy!" she screamed, and paddled hard.

Of course she was here! She'd probably been here all summer, just miles from the cabin. She'd always loved this place, had once called it her only escape from chaos. Maud leaned forward over her legs and bore down into her paddling.

But the campsite was empty and unchanged except for the red NO TRESPASSING sign nailed to a tree. Maud ripped down the sign and stuffed it into the side pouch of her pack. She was staying.

After setting up camp and eating a lunch of dried fruit and cheese, she stripped, slathered tanning lotion on as much of her backside as she could reach, then lay on a towel on the sand by the water. She loved the feeling of the sun parching her skin and seeping into her muscles. It drugged her, and she slept.

After an hour of dreamless rest, Maud was roused by the sharp bite of a mosquito on her rump. She rose and walked into the water. Afternoon naps left her groggy; immersion in cold lake water always charged her senses. She dove, then swam through the clear water with open eyes. Perch and sunfish scattered. She burst through the surface and shook her head. Wiping her eyes, she checked the sun's position above the trees. Midafternoon.

"Maud!"

She spun around and looked across the water.

Keller waved from the bow of a canoe and then resumed paddling. She identified Steve in the stern.

"What are you doing here?" she said angrily when they drew near.

"Do you always skinny-dip when you go camping?"

"Keller."

They let the canoe glide toward the shore. Keller stepped out before it could scrape against the sandy bottom. Maud back-paddled to cover herself in darker, deeper water. Steve lay back against the stern plate and rested.

"They found Lucy," said Keller. "Your dad called about two hours after you left. He said to wait to tell you until you got back on Thursday, but I knew you'd want to know." He closed his eyes and turned his back. "Get dressed."

Maud got out of the water and wrapped herself in a towel. "Where is she?"

"Are you decent?"

"I'm fine."

He faced her. "Maud, she's dead."

Tell me everything, she said.

I've told you all I know, he answered.

Tell me again. Where did it happen and who was she with?

I told you, he said. In Minneapolis, at the university, and she was with two others. Only Lucy is dead. The others left before the bomb went off. She stayed behind.

Why didn't they make her leave? she asked.

I don't know, he answered. Now just paddle. Dad's waiting with the car at the landing. We'll get you back home, and then you'll hear more.

Tell me again.

I've told you all your dad told us. It's all he knows.

Again, she said.

This morning at dawn Lucy and two guys broke into a building at the university. They got into a physics laboratory and set a bomb. Then they left.

Lucy didn't leave, she said.

She returned, he answered. She went back to the lab and called the police.

What did she say? she asked.

I told you. "I'm done running" was what she said to the police. They told your father that then she dropped the phone. A second later they heard the explosion.

Maud leaned into her paddling. Paddling was methodical, rhythmic. She loved paddling. Dip, pull, swing. Dip, pull, swing.

Tell me again.

Keller's father was waiting at the landing. He'd been there since dropping off Keller and Steve and their canoe. He was standing at the water's edge when Maud spotted him. He walked into the water and grabbed the bow of the canoe as it glided ashore. He helped Maud step out, then embraced her. "We'll go to the cabin," he said. "You can pack up, then I'll drive you to Minneapolis."

"I can drive myself."

"That's not a good idea, Maud. You won't be thinking about driving. Keller can follow in your car."

It had taken half a day to paddle and portage to Barnum Lake. Maud returned in a twenty-minute car ride. Keller's mother was hanging up laundry on a line behind their cabin when the car drove in. She dropped a wet shirt on the ground and came running.

"Have you heard more?" asked Maud. "Tell me."

"Nothing, dear. Nothing."

Keller's mother had made cookies, and she sent them along with Maud, who held the unopened box on her lap for the entire trip to Minneapolis. It was dark when they arrived at her house. There were strange cars out front, and all the lights were on. She saw people moving through the rooms. Her father came out the front door. When he saw Maud in the car he sat down on the top step and put his head in his hands.

Maud whispered, "I want yesterday."

Midnight, and at last all the neighbors and friends and police officers but one were gone. The federal agent in charge had just arrived. He apologized for coming so late.

"We talked again to her companions. Their lawyers let us talk again. They told us more."

"Tell us," Mr. Dougherty said.

"This is what we know. We may never know everything. Lucy had been underground for over a year, moving from city to city with about six others. We

21

nearly caught her twice. In Cambridge last winter, then in Boulder this June."

"You didn't tell us," said Mr. Dougherty.

"We weren't convinced you weren't in contact, and we didn't want her to know how close we were. She returned to Minneapolis last week. Where she and the others stayed is a mystery. We caught two accomplices in a coffee shop right after the bombing. They were waiting for her. They had left the physics building separately. She was the last to go. They didn't know she hadn't actually left. She returned to the bomb. They had no idea she intended to stay with it."

"She did mean to? It wasn't an accident?" asked Mr. Dougherty.

"It wasn't an accident." He continued with details. The lab, the force of the bomb, the fire that followed, the search for remains.

Maud sat back in her chair while he talked. He couldn't tell her what she most wanted to know.

Why?

Maud remained inside when her father later escorted the agent to his car. When he returned they looked at each other without speaking. Then he shook his head, turned, and climbed slowly up the stairs.

Maud watched him. He was a stocky man, not very tall, with close-cropped graying hair. Lucy had once said that he looked more like a football coach than a poet and teacher of writing. Lucy had once said . . .

Maud turned off the living room lights. She went back to the kitchen, hungry at last, and opened the box of cookies. Someone had left the paper and the day's mail on the counter. Amidst the mayhem of the day, in the chaos of family death, some friend had seen to that little task. She sorted through the mail and found, between a light bill and a department store flyer, an envelope for her from the public library. "Overdue notice," it said under the return address. She was puzzled. She was certain she had returned all her books in June. She checked the typed address again. Yes, it was for her, not her father. Maud Dougherty. Looked again. Maud X. Dougherty.

The breath went out of her. Maud X.

She had no middle name. "X" was an old family joke.

This was from Lucy. Must be. Somehow, sometime, her sister must have walked into the library and into someone's office and stolen an envelope that would escape notice, that would slip past the postal monitor.

From Lucy.

Maud opened it slowly, aware that it was the last time she'd ever hear from her sister.

Pink paper. Maud unfolded the sheet. Yes, Lucy's writing. Two lines.

"Goddamn you," Maud said as the tears started flowing. "Only two lines."

Just tell them this: they must count
me when they add up all the dead.

· 3 ·

Maud leaned over Lucy and gently slapped her cheeks. "Are you okay?" Slap, slap. "What a stupid thing to do! Now answer me, okay?" Slap, slap. "You never could dive, but you just had to try it off a twelve-foot boulder." Slap, slap. "World's best belly flop, stupid, you stupid." Slap, slap. "Now look at me!" And Lucy's eyelids fluttered open, revealing empty sockets. Maud gasped, then slapped and slapped, left and right, again and again, until her palms burned and stung from flailing against her sister's cold flesh.

Maud rolled to her other side, and her arm was unpinned. Blood rushed to her hand and the stinging pinpricks mellowed. She opened her eyes and they started adjusting to the gray light. Her window was partially covered with brown and yellow leaves, each one slapped and pasted against the glass by an adhesive of rain and wind.

For a sleepy moment she believed it was summer again and she was back at the cabin. She and her father had gone to the lake the previous weekend and, while there, her dreams of her sister had been especially vivid. It had been the first visit since Lucy's death, and it would be the last. They had decided to sell the cabin.

"I'll have a buyer within a week," the real-estate agent had said happily. "If you're really sure."

"We're certain," said Mr. Dougherty, and Maud nodded agreement. "We'll let it go. Cheap."

"Bad enough to come here without your mother all these years," he had said later to Maud.

"And now it's missing Lucy," she answered.

A gust of wind shook the house, and more leaves were slapped against the window. No maple or aspen, just city elm and ash. She was at home.

Maud heard her father's steps on the stairs. When there was no sound she closed her eyes and didn't move. She knew he was at her bedroom door.

"Go to school today, Maud," he whispered. A wish, not a command.

She waited until she heard the sound of his car driving down the alley, then sat up. The movement started a churning in her stomach. Her tongue seemed to be drawn back in her mouth and wrapped in dry cotton. She dressed, fumbling sleepily with the clothes. She had stayed up most of the night, burning through an entire candle, listening to music, and smoking one of the joints Keller had sent her.

"If you can't cheer up, light up," he'd written. She'd been angry at him for sending the pot through the mail. After all, how did they know the FBI wasn't still watching their mail and listening to the phones? At Lucy's memorial service the agents had been obvious

25

enough in their dark suits and sunglasses. Standing a few yards away from the crowd of nearly two hundred friends, family, and curious strangers that had gathered in the rose garden at Lake Harriet for readings and music, the feds seemed to be the only ones unmoved.

The memorial was the last occasion Maud and her father had actually seen any agents, and evidently the mail was no longer monitored because Keller was still roaming free.

As far as she knew, Maud was the last one of her friends to try smoking pot. And now her old resistance seemed silly. Plain silly not to end the day with a high. It brought sleep when nothing else could.

Her father had left rolls in the kitchen. Maud picked one up and examined the bottom. It was a soft golden brown, one of his better batches. He'd been experimenting with whole wheat lately, but was usually unhappy with the results. Maud often sat and watched him work in the kitchen. It was easy to talk about cooking. Though he willingly did his share in the kitchen, baking was the only cooking he actually liked to do. "So tactile," he'd explained one afternoon while punching down dough.

Maud took a bite of the roll, and immediately her stomach went into high gear. She debated smoking another joint because that often settled her stomach, but decided against it, in case she did go to school.

The stomach troubles had begun when school resumed, and they flared intermittently but often violently. Maud lost eight pounds. Her father had finally coaxed her into seeing a doctor. During the consultation that followed a series of tests, they had both laughed outright when the doctor said he could find no physical ailment and had asked if there had been any recent family problems. He had leaned forward, stroking his wispy goatee. "Perhaps some emotional upsets?"

"Well, yes," Mr. Dougherty responded after they stopped laughing at the understatement. "Something like that." Counseling was advised.

The rain had stopped, but Maud still pulled on a plastic poncho before leaving the house. A gray sheet was peeling back from a blue sky. She got her bicycle out of the garage and walked it down the driveway. When she was a little girl she had loved to ride down the steep drive and alley, leaning hard as she attempted to make the sharp turn from the alley into the street. Now she walked, the few times she even took her bicycle.

It was the second day this week she had skipped school. She liked to skip on beautiful days. But today, even if the rain hadn't stopped, it was important to be home when the mail arrived at noon because she needed to intercept her midterm grades. She didn't think it would help her father's frame of mind to see that for the first time ever she wasn't pulling straight A's. Or any A's. Or anything resembling an A.

She took back streets until she reached Franklin Avenue, then she followed that until it met the River Parkway. Three minutes later she was on the campus of the University of Minnesota and riding carefully, dodging the students who were walking alone, in pairs, in loud groups. When she reached the mall she walked her bike because the stream of students was too heavy.

When she reached the physics building she set her bike against the stump of an elm tree, took off her poncho, and spread it on the ground. She sat down. Men on scaffolds were working on the repairs, and men on the ground smoked cigarettes and joked. The large plywood patches had been removed since she'd been here two days ago. She guessed they were at last preparing to replace the windows. Maud pulled a foil package from the pouch of her sweatshirt and unwrapped a roll. She took a small bite and munched as she watched the workers measure and patch and shout and joke and put things back together.

A student with his parents in tow stopped in front of the building. He pointed, the mother shook her head, the father took a picture. ". . . get your hair cut," Maud overheard as the trio walked past her. She wondered if the mother perhaps believed that with that ordinary admonition she could somehow ensure that *her* child wouldn't die blowing up buildings.

Maud finished the roll, but before the final bite even reached the back of her tongue her stomach twisted. She lay down on the poncho, hugged her abdomen, and fell asleep.

A falling leaf tickled her cheek, stirring her enough to be disturbed by the soft murmur of a nearby conversation. Maud sat up and checked her watch. A twenty-minute nap. She hoped she hadn't slept with her mouth open.

"Studying hard?"

Maud turned to the voice and smiled at the two young women seated nearby. "Just tired," she answered.

The older girls resumed their own conversation. One of them pointed at the physics building. "There goes the first window. It's taken them long enough." "They had to match the brick," her companion said. "They did a good job."

Maud was torn. She wanted to hear what they'd say next, but she didn't think she could bear it. She hardly ever could, but she always wanted to listen.

"I guess the body was in little burnt pieces blown all over, except the head. I heard they could bury the head."

Maud rose.

"I mean, I'm against the war, too, but what she did makes no sense."

Maud picked up the poncho, folded it neatly, and placed it in her bike basket.

"Randy knows someone who had a class with her a few years ago. I guess we're talking really strange."

Maud walked away. This is 1969, she wanted to say to them. Your bouffant hairdos are what's really strange.

People were gathered in front of the student union, listening to a man who was shouting through a bullhorn. A girl handed Maud a red leaflet.

STOP WORK

STOP SCHOOL

STOP WAR

MORATORIUM OCTOBER 15

Maud folded the paper and put it in her basket. Various antiwar and peace groups, in an unusual display of unity, had been organizing since late summer for the demonstration, which would coincide with other rallies across the country. Several of the protest leaders had repeatedly called Maud and her father. Would they come? Could he speak, read a poem? The hero's family, they should be there. Others called to say just the opposite, that because Lucy chose weapons of violence she was no hero, and her family should stay away.

Maud left the crowd at the union and got sucked into the flow of students moving among buildings between classes. The campus was divided in two by the Mississippi River, and a double-decker bridge — pedestrians above, vehicles below — connected the east and west sides. Maud mounted her bike and rode onto the bike lane on the bridge. She had a large bulb horn screwed onto the handlebars, and she honked it twice at walkers who strayed into her path.

She rode past orange-brick classroom buildings, past the new library, and through two parking lots. Then she was off the campus and in a neighborhood of run-down houses and businesses. She parked her bike in a rack behind a vegetarian cafeteria. At the memorial service several people had mentioned how they'd heard Lucy had been spotted on the West Bank only a few days before she died. Dressed in green, dressed in army fatigues, spotted wearing yellow. No one really could say. It made sense to Maud that Lucy and her companions had ended up in this neighborhood. It was full of wishful people: those who wished they lived in San Francisco, those who wished they were still in college, or wished they were dancers, or artists, or writers, or revolutionaries.

A bus roared past on Riverside Avenue, its exhaust washing over her. Maud held her breath, but when she filled her lungs again there was diesel residue in the air and immediately her stomach churned.

"Maud, you should be in school!"

Maud turned and looked with surprise at a tall, skinny man wearing a tie-dyed caftan. A striped headband was wrapped twice around, and the ends dangled to his shoulders. She choked on a laugh. "Hello, Mr. Randall." Her history teacher. "You should be, too."

He lifted his arms, and the voluminous sleeves swished. "Not on a day like this. I couldn't stomach all that bullshit today. Treaty of Ghent, Missouri Compromise — none of that matters, does it, Maud? I called in sick today, but you know" — he frowned and stepped closer — "I may have to quit. It's all so irrelevant."

She murmured something. He accepted that as an agreement. He took her hands in his and lifted them to his chest. She bit her cheeks to keep from smiling.

31

Mr. Randall was a first-year teacher, and he looked younger than many of his students. "Call me Rod, Maud."

She smiled. "Sure. Rod."

"Let's go to Richter's. Let's see what's happening."

She let him guide her down the street. He wrapped his arm across her back and hugged. His hand began to move up and down. The thumb thumped repeatedly across her bra strap, while the tips of his fingers, curled around her side, grazed the edge of her breast. Rod had an eager bounce to his walk — a sign, Maud figured, of a happy man liberated by the illicit acts of skipping school, hugging a student, and copping a feel.

Maud tried not to think about how weird it was to be hooked up with a teacher. Instead, she aped his walk, and by the time they reached the drugstore she was almost infected with his buoyant mood.

Richter's Drug was a meeting spot for the varied residents of the West Bank. All the students, former students, hippies, and even many old-timers gathered on the sidewalk in front of the store to hear news, leave messages, find out how and where to score some dope. A small crowd had assembled and was listening to music. A man was playing a hammered dulcimer. Tan and muscular, he wore blue-jean cutoffs that had embroidered rainbows on the front pockets, and he was shirtless under an unzipped army jacket. He swayed slightly as he stood behind his instrument and tapped the strings.

Maud pulled her sweater cuffs down over her

wrists, shivered, and wondered how he could stand the cool October air. He seemed truly oblivious to the chill, though she noticed his nipples were stiff. His nerds were perked, her friends would say. While he tapped out a melody, she watched and listened, obsessed with a new thought: why do guys even have nipples? Before she could figure it out, she was bumped from behind, and she turned to look. People were dancing, and a woman with a baby on her shoulder smiled apologetically at Maud. Rod's hand stroked faster.

The red leaflets were being distributed. Rod took several and tucked them into his backpack. "I'll pass them out in school tomorrow," he said. "Everyone should go, we should close down the high school. They say there will be millions protesting across the whole country."

In front of them, a woman turned around. "There will be buses going to the march in Washington," she said. "We hope to send several hundred people."

"No!" Rod barked. "Local action, grass-roots strength — that's what we need."

The two bent their heads together and argued. Maud slipped away and moved around the edge of the crowd. She watched as an old woman came out of the store, gathered her loaded shopping bag to her chest, and then pushed her way through.

"Out, out," the woman muttered, as if she were chasing an unwanted dog from her kitchen. She turned down the sidewalk, still muttering.

The musician concluded a song, and people applauded. Maud started to leave but was stopped as Rod slipped his arm through hers. "Got you!" he said, and grinned. He nodded toward the man behind him. "This is Ed. And this is the girl, this is Lucy Dougherty's sister. Ed and I," he said to Maud, "had a class together at Grinnell before he dropped out. What class was it, Ed? French philosophers? Yeah — no! Nihilism in Art. No, maybe . . ." He rubbed his chin as he searched his memory.

Ed ignored him. He stared at Maud as he took a drag on his cigarette. He was short and solid and hairy. Unkempt dark curls spilled over his head, cascading into a full beard. Chest hair poked out of the neck of his sweatshirt.

He exhaled a long stream of smoke. "Two nights before the bombing, Lucy and the others came to our place."

Maud tensed. Rod was chatting, lost in his college reminiscence. They ignored him.

"It was so beautiful, she was so incredible, man. We all stayed up the whole night. No one let on what was being planned. She and one guy even said they were taking off for Mexico the next morning. She'd been hiding in a farmhouse."

"Where, did she say where?"

He shrugged. "Near Northfield. No one knew what they were gonna do. It was all so easy and free the whole night. All the talk. She recited this poem, and we were like all knocked out by it. Then she wrote the thing on a wall. She left it for us. It's sort of a shrine.

Nancy keeps some flowers there. She's one of my roommates."

"What poem?"

"I don't know. I thought it was one of hers."

"She didn't write poetry, but our father does. Could I see it?"

"Sure. I'll take you there now."

Rod had finally shut up and he stared with an open mouth as they walked away, his imagined opportunity to score with a student disappearing on the arm of an old college friend.

Ed's apartment was a block off Cedar Avenue above a bar. He led her around the back of the building to steps. Maud eyed them suspiciously; several rungs were missing. "There are six of us living here now," said Ed. "Everyone shares. It's pretty cool." He led her up the steps. At the top he unlocked and opened a door, and a cat ran out. Ed reached to grab it, then shrugged. "That's your trip, Che. Go ahead and find some bus wheels."

They entered through a kitchen. Maud wrinkled her nose at the stale air that was mixed with the odor of grease and onions. She felt rumblings in her stomach. Ed led her into a hall. "Here," he said. "This is it. It's so beautiful."

Had her sister actually written a poem, maybe left it as a message that would explain something, anything? Or maybe she'd copied one of their father's, perhaps one of the sonnets Lucy had always despised as too romantic.

Maud knelt and traced over the scrawled words with her finger. Ed stood close behind, his knee pressed against her buttocks. She read to herself. "Things fall apart; the centre cannot hold;/Mere anarchy is loosed upon the world . . ." She stopped, then rose and turned. "It's Yeats."

"What's yates?"

"He's an Irish writer. Dead."

Ed leaned against the wall. "That night was so beautiful. She was funny one minute, then she'd say something serious and true. No one knew that two days later she'd be dead. She was just eating with us and talking and doing the poem thing. She and I danced. Someone put on Nina Simone, and Lucy wanted to dance. It was a slow, slow song." He smiled and stepped closer to Maud. "You look a lot like her, you know that?" His thumb caressed her brow. "Same black hair. Same blue eyes."

"Who was she with? Who were her friends?"

"There were a bunch of them, maybe four or five. Man, this one guy was wild about her. Temple, one of the guys the cops caught in the coffee shop. You could tell they had something special going. I let them use my room, you know, because by dawn, after listening to her all night he was just wild. They were there for a couple of hours before they split."

Maud let him kiss her, let his arms envelop her. She pressed her face against his chest. He had a warm, sweet, moist smell. Nice. Had Lucy noticed and enjoyed it while dancing?

She let him lead her into his room. "Tell me more,"

she whispered as he peeled off her shirt and bra and scraped his bearded face against her breasts. Tell me what she wore and said and drank. Tell me if she smiled and who else she kissed and what she ate for supper. Tell me: did she mention my name?

Ed had a poster of Chairman Mao taped to the ceiling above his bed. As he rocked and grunted, Maud locked eyes with the Chinese leader. Had Lucy lain here and done the same?

The sex couldn't have been easy for Ed, she realized when he was quiet, pushing in hard the way he'd had to. Maybe not even that pleasurable, though he had moaned happily when he rolled off. Maud immediately crossed her legs and pressed them together, but still it ached and stung.

Ed lit a joint and offered it to Maud. She shook her head.

Ed sucked, held his breath, let it out. "Too much," he whispered. "I made it with Lucy D's sister. Her own sister." He rolled his head and looked at Maud. "Jesus, what did you say your name was? I gotta tell the others. Lucy D's sister."

Maud stood. She dressed without speaking.

Ed pushed up on an elbow. "You mad?"

She buttoned the last button. "It's Maud," she whispered. "Lucy D's sister is named Maud."

He looked at his joint, put it to his lips, then inhaled again. "She was just so beautiful," he said through a clenched jaw.

Che, the cat, walked in when she opened the door. Maud ran down the steps, nearly tripping twice where

37

the rungs were gone. She didn't look behind to see if Ed had followed to protest her hasty departure. But probably he hadn't, probably he was still lying on the bed, drifting in a haze of daydream and smoke. Maud hoped she'd left blood on his sheets.

She reclaimed her bicycle and quickly rode through campus. She nearly slammed into a couple who stopped abruptly on the bridge to embrace and kiss. She swerved around them, and they broke apart and shouted at her.

She bounced over a curb to get onto the parkway, and the bicycle seat slammed against her aching crotch. She peddled furiously to maintain speed as she climbed a hill.

She was halted by a red light at Franklin Avenue. On the other side of the street a large cluster of university students waited to cross. As she balanced with one foot on the ground and caught her breath, Maud looked at each of them. She knew many of them would walk down the mall past the physics building and have something to say about Lucy's death. There'd be speculation about the body pieces, or the sense of it all, or comments on the nice job the workmen were doing. Some would question Lucy's sanity, and some would paint her a hero. Some would hate, some would admire, one or two might even lust after the dead woman's sister.

The light changed, and Maud crossed. She stared at the ground as she passed the others. Go to the mall and look, all of you, she thought. And in case you want to know, there was nothing left to bury.

A public death. She'd lost her sister in a public death. In a single bright explosion her sister, her canoe companion, her friend had been turned over to the gawkers and philosophers. Lucy had been claimed and taken.

When she reached the curb Maud turned and watched the backs of the students — so many of them laughing — and a fear rooted in her. She understood then that slowly and surely her knowledge and memory of Lucy would be displaced by other people's opinions and longings and by the simple, horrid image of how she had died.

By the time she reached home her stomach was hurting again, tighter than ever, and she moaned for it to unwind. She rushed into the house and raced into the bathroom. She calmed herself by kneeling over the toilet and listening to the amplified breathing in the porcelain bowl. She tried not to think of Ed and what she'd let him do.

The phone rang, and she ignored it. Probably no one — a crank call, some angry Gold Star Mother, a reporter. Friends sometimes called, but Maud no longer partied or even wanted to see them, and already they were drifting away. She didn't blame them.

People from the peace groups called frequently. The last time someone called to request that Maud's father speak at a teach-in, he'd slammed down the phone and angrily turned to Maud. "They all think they understand what she was doing," he said. "One way or another, they've got it figured out. My daughter's death, they've got it figured out."

Sister's death. Maud rose and went into the kitchen. She sat on a stool at the counter and fingered the morning newspaper. The front page was a black-and-white listing of sad news. At the bottom she spotted the usual Pentagon update, boxed in thick black lines: 95 killed last week, 363 last month, 8,270 year-to-date.

"No," she said. "Eight thousand two hundred seventy-*one*."

She made it to the bathroom in a fast slide that ended with her head over the bowl as she lost what seemed like everything she'd ever eaten. When her mouth was dry and her heart had resumed a normal pace she rose, went to her room, and lay on her bed. She hugged a pillow and looked out the window. She wondered if Ed had returned to Richter's and rejoined that constant crowd of the unrooted to announce that he'd bedded Lucy D's sister. She wondered about her history teacher, gleeful and bouncy in his silly caftan. Would he enjoy the news of the seduction of Lucy D's sister?

Maud turned over and fell asleep. By the time she woke, the sun had slipped around two corners of the house. She was nudged out of her sleep by the slight bouncing of her mattress.

"Hey, Maudie," her father whispered.

She woke fully. Damn, she thought. She hadn't gotten the mail. She pushed up on an elbow. "You're home early."

"No, it's nearly five."

Maud sat up and clamped her hands on her thighs. Could he tell? Did she smell? Would his heart crack and die if she told him her newest secret?

He set a mug and plate on her bedside table. "I made you some tea and toast. You haven't eaten all day, have you?"

"One of your rolls. It was a good batch." She didn't want to say that it hadn't stayed down.

"Drink this and eat the toast. You'll feel better." He curled and recurled both hands into fists, then set them on his knees. "Maud, your progress report arrived."

She looked at him straight on for the first time since waking. "I'm sorry. I'm so sorry."

He smoothed back her hair, and Maud lightly touched his hand. She wondered at the strangeness of the feeling, then realized it had been a long time since he had touched her so. Her father had always been an affectionate man, but at some time — her mother's death? Lucy's disappearance? — his gestures and words of love had thinned to nothing. Maud guessed that he was channeling the turbulent and painful emotions to his written words.

"Maud," he said as his hand rested and cupped her neck. "I think sometimes . . ." He looked at the window. She sensed he'd been pulled elsewhere.

"What?" she prompted.

"I think about Lucy, just sitting there and waiting. What was she thinking about, those last moments?"

"I've wanted to know that, too."

"What I most want to understand is whether she died with a martyr's passion or because she no longer believed in anything at all."

She could feel the arterial pulsing in her neck under his hand. She slipped her fingers under his and squeezed. He smiled at her.

"Dad, I was over on the West Bank today and I talked with someone who met her just a couple of days before she died. She came to a dinner at his place with a bunch of people. He told me she'd said she'd been hiding on a farm near Northfield. But then she also told everyone she was leaving for Mexico when really she was planning the bombing. I suppose she had to lie to be safe. Evidently she sat around this greasy apartment and talked the whole night. She could have been caught, Dad. Someone could have just called and told the cops where she was. I wish someone had."

"Maybe she trusted them."

"She could have trusted me."

"Not really. Not as long as the men in blue cars were parked out front. What else did this guy say about her?"

Ed's enthralled expression as he spoke about Lucy was vivid in Maud's mind. She closed her eyes, and still it loomed, like a distorted cartoon balloon floating overhead. She looked at her father. "She ate supper. She danced. She quoted Yeats."

He grinned. "No!"

"This guy" — this stupid, hairy jerk, this man with

a sweet warm smell — "this guy thought it was her own poetry. He was sort of in love with her."

"She hated Yeats. Always called him a romantic Irish travel writer. Got it all wrong, of course. Did he say which poem?"

"I saw it. I went with him and I saw it. She wrote it on the wall and put *her* name underneath, 'A gift from Lucy Dougherty.' Another lie."

"Which poem?"

She fingered the edge of her blanket, liking the sharp feel of it underneath her nail. " 'The blood-dimmed tide is loosed . . . ,' " she whispered, then her mouth dried and her stomach twisted. "It was 'The Second Coming.' " She lifted one hand to her mouth and grabbed her abdomen with the other. She took long, slow breaths until it all stilled.

"Oh, Maudie, maybe it's time to see a counselor."

Maud slapped her knee. "No. That won't fix it, Dad. It can't be fixed. She, she . . ."

He waited. He picked up a charred incense stick and rolled it through his fingers like a baton.

"Dad, I go over to campus and I look at the building and I listen to people, and all I can think about is how much she destroyed. She ruined so much. She lied and she destroyed."

They locked eyes, and she could see how empty his seemed, drained of hope by the weighty fact of a child's death. Then his eyes widened, hardened, darkened. "*I* am not destroyed," he whispered. "And neither are you." He kissed her. "Don't, Maud. Don't let your life be held hostage to her death."

He rose and left. She could hear him climb the steps to his third-floor study. It was his retreat, where he'd go to write or think, to look out the window or look within. She wondered what he had written since August. Wondered what poems came flowing from or were blocked within his pen.

She remembered how he used to sing his poems to her and Lucy. At the lake they would often sit on the dock and he would recite his newest poem, one that had taken days or weeks to write and shape. Then he'd put those words on top of music made up at that very moment. That's how they had learned to look at the lake and trees and the never-ending, mind-teasing, star-studded northern sky: with their father's arms and poetry and music wrapped around them.

Maud sipped some tea and bit into the toast. The tea was made of mint from the garden. She finished the toast and drained the mug, and her stomach relaxed immediately. He was right, she felt better. Now, if he could only promise her that the sadness wouldn't be everlasting.

• *Part II* •

Body Count

· 1 ·

Third beer of my life. Three beers in seventeen years. Not that it was any big thing, or that my mother is hard-nosed about drinking. As a matter of fact, all she's ever said on the subject to me and my brother is, "Don't be stupid about it, boys." Still, it is illegal, so I generally don't do it. But I felt like celebrating. At this afternoon's student council meeting I had stood up in front of all those school stars, all those king jocks and cheerleaders and merit scholars, and requested that they consider passing a resolution I'd written condemning the war in Vietnam. After some debate — it was a little heated, but not nearly as bad as it could have been — the resolution was passed. It helped, I think, that most kids my age don't like Nixon. And it especially helped that my best friend, Gumbo, who's the most popular guy on the council because he brings Rice Krispie treats to all the meetings, threatened to never again bring treats unless the resolution was passed. People laughed, but voted yes. Of course, I don't want to give Gum too much credit. It's May, and there's only one meeting left. People couldn't have been too concerned about their treats. I hope.

Whatever the reasons, the resolution passed, to my extreme surprise. I live in Red Cedar, Minnesota, which has got to be the world's most conservative town. It's the kind of place where the whole town shows up at the cemetery on Memorial Day for speeches and grave-decorating, a town where flags fly on holidays, and where, as July approaches, all the ladies get into red, white, and blue craft projects. Come Independence Day, the homes in my town are decorated in patriotic needlepoint.

That kind of fervor can rub off on the kids, which is why I was surprised today when they voted through the resolution. Of course, it's 1969 and the rest of the country has been protesting for a couple of years already, but, hey, why complain? It passed.

And I had made it happen, and I was proud. So why not have a beer? Just one, of course. I didn't want to be stupid about it. I got the bottle out of the fridge, rolled it in my hands for a moment, then popped the cap. After a long, slow chug I sat down and started singing an old Bob Dylan song.

I'm not real good with lyrics, so all I could remember was the chorus, which I repeated over and over. I was on about the tenth round when my brother, Tom, walked into the kitchen. He headed for the refrigerator and his own beer, but he stopped in the middle of the room, goal forgotten, and looked hard at me.

"Yeah?" I said, waiting to be told to shut up.

"Holy Cow, Jeff," he said. He was just out of the shower, naked except for a towel, and was still damp and mottled red from the scalding water he preferred.

"Do you realize that your voice would be great for getting dates? Do you realize that girls are suckers for a sexy, low voice? You should take advantage of it. When's the last time you went out?"

I shook my head. The biggest day of my life, and this clown brings it down to dating.

"C'mon, when's the last time you went out?" he repeated.

I'd never gone out, not the way he meant. But I knew he wouldn't understand that, wouldn't understand how much things had changed in the years since he'd been a high school senior. Back in 1963, at least from what I could observe from my brother, the acknowledged high priest of dating, there were real formal patterns of social behavior. Not now.

He took a drink, swallowed, then squinted at me. "You're a junior. You can go to prom this spring. You going? You got a date? Hell, Jeff, do you even know how to dance?"

I had to laugh, I just had to. Dance. That was another big difference between '63 and '69. Back then they actually danced. No one I know dances now. Okay, maybe if the music is right and people are loaded they'll get up and move around. But it's nothing my brother or his friends would recognize as dancing. These days, no one dances and no one dates. The closest we get to dating, I suppose, is to go with a crowd of friends to the armory to listen to whatever band is down from Minneapolis. You know you're with someone for the night if you share a soft drink and hold hands during the drum solo.

When I didn't say anything, not wanting to explain about the armory and drum solos and how I hadn't really been planning on dancing, he shook his head vigorously. "A voice like yours and it goes to waste. Like I said, Jeff, you gotta take advantage of what you have."

"I'm not sure what you mean," I said. That was a lie, of course. Growing up with my brother was a daily lesson in taking advantage of what you had. In his case, what he had was a great body; the word "physique" was invented for guys like Tom. I may have had the voice, but he had the body for getting dates.

He tapped on the table to make sure I was listening. "What I mean is that any girl will do anything you want as long as you use that voice to whisper the request in a dark room."

"Anything?"

"Guaranteed."

"Then maybe I should call one up and ask her to get me a cookie out of the cupboard." I pointed across the kitchen. "Or maybe my big brother would do it for me."

He got me the cookie, but I could tell he wasn't amused. He shook his head slowly while he debated if I was a lost cause. Water dripped off his forelock onto his nose. He wiped it off, but made a mistake and used the hand that was securing the towel around his waist. It fell to the ground just as our mother walked in the back door with her date, Paul Sanborn. Mom was unfazed by the sight of her naked son standing in the kitchen, but Paul wheeled around and fiddled with his tie.

I kicked the towel into the air. Tom grabbed it and trotted out of the kitchen to the bedroom we shared when he was home on leave.

My mother flipped her hand in the air. "My sons," she said. I wasn't sure if she meant it as an introduction or a complaint. Complaint, I suppose, because she knew I had already met Paul. He was a foreman in Mom's department at Porter's Pork Processing, *the* company in this one-company town. Mom and Paul both worked in vacuum pack, where all the bacon, ham, and sausage gets sealed up.

"Why are you home?" I asked her. Friday night was her time to relax, and she usually stayed out late.

"We met Ginny and Gerry at the lodge, and they said come on over for cards. They buy cheap booze, so I made Paul stop so's I could get my own bottle." She squatted and reached into the bottom cupboard. She was wearing a tight powder-blue dress. It slid up, revealing the dark strip at the top of her nylon that was gripped by the little round thing at the bottom of her garter strap. Paul must have seen the same thing because we both real fast averted our gaze and then were caught looking at each other. Mom pulled out a quart of Johnnie Walker Black. She looked hard at it for a moment, then turned to Paul. "Think one will do?"

My mother had lived all of her forty-seven years in different parts of Waltham County, Minnesota, but, according to my father, she drank like a Texan. My dad, a Lubbock native who'd wandered north once with a semitrailer full of hogs destined for baconhood at the plant, met her at a bar in Red Cedar. He claimed that her vivacity on the dance floor and with a bottle made him homesick, and he proposed before the night was out. She accepted, liking the fact that he quickly agreed to her conditions: they'd stay in town, and she'd keep working at the plant. Besides, as she often explained to herself and others who questioned her hastiness in marrying a stranger from Texas, it was 1945 and people were just lining up to get married. She wasn't going to miss that.

Paul convinced her that only one bottle was necessary. She stuffed it into her bag and slung that over her shoulder just as Tom returned to the kitchen. He had date clothes on: khakis, light-blue oxford-cloth shirt, no socks, and high-polished loafers.

"Num-num," Mom said, looking at him. "Who's the lucky one tonight?"

"Sheila Sartell. Double date." He nodded at me. "With Jeffie. He's taking out Pete Whippet's sister Tess."

"Huh?" I said, my good-for-dates voice barking out like a seal's. "Since when?"

Mom looked back and forth between us. She had blue eyes like mine, but when she beamed in and looked for something below the surface the way she was now, her eyes lost all color and went ice-cool. She settled on my big brother. "Don't, Tommy. Don't make him do anything he doesn't want to."

"Yeah, Tommy," I added, and grinned. One thing

we had learned long ago was that whoever got Mom on his side almost always won.

Paul shifted in the background. "Connie?" he said tentatively. "Let's go?"

I smiled at him. He was like most guys my mom had dated since the divorce — tall, good-looking, in charge of something at the plant, but in charge of nothing when with my mother.

She reached back to pat his hand, only she missed and swiped his crotch. He stepped back, put his hands in his pockets, and jingled coins and keys.

"How did it go today?" she asked me.

"Fine. It passed." I glanced nervously at my brother.

"Did you tell Tom?" she asked.

"No."

"I think you should tell him. If —"

"Tell me what?"

She kept her gaze on me. "— if you're going to do these things you shouldn't hide them from your brother. He'll find out, anyway, as soon as he gets to whatever party he's going to tonight. He should hear it from you." She turned to Paul. "Two boys. Same father, same mother, same house, same goldarn tuna casseroles. Two boys, and you'd never know they were related."

I smiled. It was a familiar observation.

She wagged a finger at Tom. "Leave him alone, Tommy. You know he's not one for dating, and besides, I don't want you to push him into going out with any girl *you* know."

My brother had been a high school athletic star whom people in Red Cedar still talked about six years after his graduation. And he was a lovable, gorgeous, generous son who remembered birthdays and Mother's Days and even made up other occasions to celebrate with gifts and flowers. Every mother's dream boy. But our mother had always made it clear that as different as Tom and I were, she knew she had two dream boys.

That thought was why she never bad-mouthed my father, not through the married years when he had a string of girlfriends, not after the divorce when he drove off and disappeared inside Texas. Not a single bad word. "I got you two out of Herb," she'd said often enough. "That means I owe him."

She jabbed the starched shoulder of Tom's shirt. "Stay home tomorrow. It's your last full day of leave, and I want us all to have dinner at the Oak Leaf. And I warn you, Tommy, leave him be." She turned and left. Paul followed, still jingling the contents of his pockets.

I got up to empty my nearly full bottle into the sink, but Tom halted me by clamping his hands on my shoulders. I was as tall as my brother, six-foot-one, but thirty pounds lighter, and I rocked under his touch. "What's she talking about?"

I turned and poured. Foamy gold liquid swirled around the drain grid before disappearing.

"Jeff?"

I faced him. "I offered a resolution today for the

54

student council's consideration. It was passed. It was about Vietnam."

He nodded slowly, set his beer down, then crossed his arms and tucked his hands under his armpits. His biceps bulged, causing the oxford cloth to strain. His body had been shaped by years of athletics, then perfected by four years of Marine Corps drill. Still, I guess I had the voice.

"Maybe it's time we talk," he said. "Maybe it's time we talk about that peace-sign poster you put up in our bedroom that I have to look at every time I come home on leave. Maybe it's time to talk about all those liberal magazines you leave lying around. And about the things friends tell me about my little brother."

"It was a resolution condemning U.S. involvement in Vietnam."

"Somehow that doesn't surprise me. Maybe it's time we do talk, about whether or not you think your brother is, oh, what is it they call us? Baby-killers? Why don't you say it?"

"I don't think that about you, Tom."

"But only because I haven't yet been to Vietnam, right? Well, that oughta change real soon." He finished his bottle in a fast, angry gulp, then wiped his mouth with the back of his hand.

"Tom, I don't want to fight about this. My argument with the war has nothing to do with you or any other guy in uniform."

"That's crap. If you hate the war you hate the guys

who do the fighting. You can't separate us from the dirty deed, little brother."

"I can separate you. Let's not fight, Tom. Do you really want to fight?"

I knew the answer. Neither of us did, which was why neither had ever mentioned anything about the poster I'd put up in the room two years ago, or maybe why we never watched news together when he was home, or why the only things we talked about in the paper were the baseball scores and the funnies. Family peace sometimes means a little judicious silence.

He gave me a small smile. "Same goldarn casseroles, huh?"

"Something."

His smile widened. "The way I look at it, you owe me."

"What?"

"You owe me. So go on the date, Jeff. Tess is a sweet thing, and not that much older than you."

I couldn't believe it, couldn't believe that he had swung from a family fight over the Vietnam War to dating. I stiffened. "I had plans." That wasn't exactly true, but there was usually something going on. I knew at least I could rustle up Gumbo, and if he wasn't too stoned we'd go to a movie or find a party or hang out at the Country Café. Like I said, I had plans.

"I can guess your plans. You and Gumbo, right? Only now, instead of riding bikes to the candy store or going fishing at the river, you'll probably drive around getting stoned. Forget it, Jeff. You owe me. Just call up Tess and ask her out."

"I don't do drugs, Tom."

"So you say, but it's not what I hear, at least not about your best friend. I hear he's into some heavy stuff."

I couldn't deny that. Gumbo lived across the street, and at one time we'd been closer to each other than either of us was to his own brother. But lately Gum, like lots of kids I knew, had started doing some serious partying, way wilder than what I cared for. "I guess that's something else I don't want to fight about, Tom. Look, I'm beat. Besides, it's seven on a Friday night. I don't know much dating protocol, but wouldn't it be insulting to call a girl on such late notice?"

"It's never insulting to be asked out."

"I don't know her." Worse, she didn't know me. I didn't want to face anyone's disappointment. I don't look much like my brother. I can't say for certain what I do look like, but it probably wouldn't be wrong to use Tom's old description of a telephone pole with a dinkus.

"You don't need to know her. She knows *me*. Don't be tough on me, Jeffie. You're going to do this. You're going to go to the phone and ask her out, and we're all going to a party at Dan's, where you will spend a night in the company of people who aren't dopeheads. After I'm gone, you can mess around with your crowd and pretend you're all hippies or student radicals, but not tonight. Tonight you'll take out Tess, go to the party, dance with her, neck with her, meet some other real girls, and put down a foundation for when I'm not around to get you dates. You're not gonna stay at home planning some other dumb-ass resolution and then put yourself to sleep reading some dumb-ass German writer."

"Cool it, Tom."

"We're going out. You know why?"

"Why, Tom?"

"Because every night I've been home you've been out doing something with your liberal hippie friends. This meeting or that meeting. Hanging out at the café talking about God knows what. The first night I got back you were gone, for Chrissake. And where? At some church for a peace teach-in? I couldn't believe it when Mom told me that. And last Christmas when I was home you were away at some student council retreat. What was that all about? Nonviolence? Fighting racism? Growing your own drugs?"

"I don't do drugs, Tom. Would you get that much straight?"

He didn't hear me. He was on a tear. "In two days my leave is over and I head for Pendleton. Then I get shipped out to Nam, little brother. Four years of slipping around it, I finally get the orders. And in case I eat some gook's bullet, I want to die knowing I shared one night with my little brother. One night, Jeffrey. Vietnam. The dirty word. It's time." During his first enlistment in the Corps, Tom had avoided a tour of combat duty, managing somehow to get assigned for his overseas stint to a carrier in the Mediterranean. But then he finished his four years, tried school, failed at that, and signed up again, knowing that this time there'd be no way he'd avoid combat.

I called Tess. She seemed pleased. "I didn't know Tommy had an older brother."

"Younger brother. I'll be a high school senior next fall."

I could just about feel her chewing on that. But I suppose my voice and the reference as Tom's brother, or maybe just the horror of an empty Friday night, clinched her. "I'll be ready," she said.

I put down the phone and avoided looking at Tom.

He picked out my clothes, not trusting me to wear anything other than my usual uniform of T-shirt and old jeans with wide, ragged bells. He loaned me everything but the underwear — shirt and slacks that matched his and another pair of loafers with a military polish. Our clothing was identical, but there was no way we'd be confused as twins.

"Let's get your date first," I said when we got in the car. I had a knot in my stomach, but I was determined to play along and not complain. My head was beginning to ache, but this was his night, his farewell party. He backed out of the driveway, then shifted, hit the gas, and let the car leap forward.

Tom shook his head. "Nope," he said. "First we get gas, and then, little brother, I have to show you the best place to buy rubbers."

· 2 ·

"What makes you think I don't know how to do that? Any fool can find his way to a drugstore."

Tommy tossed his cigarette butt out the window. It hit the road and sparks flew.

"Do you mean, Jeffie, that you'd be willing to walk into Blaine's Pharmacy, go up to the counter, and ask good old Barnett for some proph-uh-lac-tics?" He veered around a corner without signaling. "Wasn't his wife your Cub Scout leader?"

"Den mother. I get your point. None of it matters, though, because I don't need anything just now."

"Maybe not now, but someday. And then you will know that this" — he thumbed toward the truck stop we were approaching — "is the place. There are no family friends behind the counter, and the machine never eats your quarters."

He nosed in behind a semi that was creeping into the truck stop, then, as soon as he had room, accelerated and swerved around it and pulled up to a pump.

"Got any money?" he said. I fished a five out of my pocket and handed it to him.

"That's for gas," I said. "I don't want you buying me anything else."

He got out and signaled to the pump attendant. "Five dollars," he said, then went into the station. I got out and stood aside while the boy worked on the windshield.

I like the smell of gas fumes. I suppose they are kind of poisonous, but it's not like I inhale the stuff with a paper bag over my head. I just like to stand by the tanks on a warm night like this one and let the fumes waft up. It conjures up so fast all these memories of traveling with my family before my dad split. Once a year we'd go to Texas — to see the real world, my dad would say. And even though his voice and face are now a little vague, when I get a headful of gas fumes I can just about feel what it was like to stand by him on the hot asphalt while we tanked up at some Skelly alongside U.S. 75 in Kansas or Oklahoma. I always liked to listen to him B.S. with other travelers or the service boy, liked to listen to that casual men's talk about baseball or crops or good spots for coffee and rolls.

The pump boy finished as Tom returned, walking fast and grinning as if he had made off with the contents of the till.

"What did you get?" I asked suspiciously.

"Five bucks of gas and" — he stopped to burrow in his pants pocket — "Juicy Fruit."

We got in the car, and Tom wasted no time. "A party is beginning," he said as he looked over his shoulder before making a squealing U-turn, "and I'm not part of the action."

His date kept him waiting for five minutes, which

he spent talking to her father. I could see the two of them through the screen door. Every now and then one or the other would say something apparently funny and they'd both tip back their heads and laugh. Parents seemed to like my brother.

I let Sheila sit in front with Tom. She scooted over next to him on the seat. From the regular, slight twitching of her shoulder I could tell that she must have been stroking his leg. Ah, Tommy.

My date was waiting at the door. She didn't seem disappointed at all to be picked up by someone young and gangly, and I gave her a real smile of appreciation.

In the car she offered me a cigarette. I shook my head. "Just smoke the illegal stuff, I suppose," she said. I gave her another good smile, but didn't answer. She kicked the back of the front seat. "Hey, Sheila, has he got your pants off yet?"

"Tess!" Sheila squealed. She avoided looking at Tom. He turned around and gave Tess a wicked grin. I could just about see his mind at work, undoubtedly figuring that maybe he'd made a mistake and fixed up his little brother with the live one.

Tess opened her purse and pulled out a flask. She offered it to me. Again I refused, and she shook her head. "You are a pure one, aren't you?"

Tom sped the car through a few yellow lights, turned off onto a side street that flanked the high school, and pulled over. "We walk from here. Looks like a mob."

Tess took my hand and pulled me out of the car. "I hope to God you at least dance," she said.

The house was packed with people who looked as if they had just been released from a time capsule sealed since 1963, the year I figured most of them had graduated from high school. The girls all looked like variations of Tess and Sheila, with the kind of hair that resembled space helmets. Most of the guys compensated with flattops. Thanks to Tom's wardrobe, I pretty much blended in, except for my hair, which covered my neck and ears. It was the first thing Danny Miller commented on when he welcomed me.

"Who brought the little hippie?" he shouted, and everyone roared. Danny hugged me then. He'd been Tom's best friend for years.

The party was to celebrate his acceptance to divinity school. He wasn't the least bit religious, but it was his last chance to avoid the draft, so he'd applied, using his years as a YMCA day-camp counselor as proof of his commitment to a life of service. I'd worked with him as a junior counselor, and I knew that mostly he'd gone to camp to avoid the usual summer employment that was available to local boys at the plant, where they would kill and gut livestock or hose down bloody work areas.

Danny kissed Tess, then whispered to her. "Bobby's here. He wants you to say hello. He's in the kitchen." She stiffened and looked at me.

"Old boyfriend," said Danny. "Be a sport and let her go, okay?"

I shrugged. "Hey, have fun." Tess hugged me before she raced to the kitchen.

"She's too much for you, anyway, schoolboy,"

Danny said. He led me around the crowd. I knew most of the people, and the guys slapped me on the back and the girls winked. There were a few strangers, and Danny introduced me to them as Tom Ramsey's kid brother, home on weekend furlough from Red Wing. Those folks usually backed up a step. Red Wing was a small town about ninety miles away and was the site of the state school for delinquent boys.

"Do that once more," I finally hissed in his ear, "and I start telling people about the time you and Tom climbed on the roof of the Congregational church, pulled down your pants, and watered the flowers."

Danny roared. "I'd forgotten!" He grabbed someone's arm. "Hey, did I ever tell you about the time this future minister . . ."

I left him and worked my way into the kitchen. Tom had vanished, and so had both of the girls. I figured I was free to leave, but I was hungry and wanted to eat first. There were sandwiches and soda and chips, and I loaded up, then carried it all back to the main room and watched the action.

People were having a good time. There was a lot of shouting and laughing and smooth dancing by couples that looked glued together. They all looked like happy people, which was kind of weird because I went to school with plenty of their brothers and sisters and no one would ever watch a party of ours and say, Wow, happy times! But, it figured. Most of these guys and girls had finished high school and gotten all their childhood over before people started getting shot and cities started burning. Maybe they didn't feel so robbed.

A short, balding, heavyset man was looking at me from across the room. He was a young guy with a serious face. He plowed through the dancers without speaking to anyone, came to me, and offered his hand. "Jeff Ramsey?"

I shook hands with him. "Yeah. You?"

"Roger Heistad." He sat down. "I'm the interim youth pastor at English Lutheran."

I stared at my sandwich. "Did Danny tell you I was on furlough from Red Wing?"

He snitched one of my chips. "No. Are you?"

"No."

"Even if you were, Jeff, you needn't worry because I don't do my soul-saving at parties. I heard about you from Maggie Hewitt. I've been meaning to call you."

Now I was interested. Maggie was a senior, or used to be a senior, and had been on the student council with me. She'd been suspended twice for leading demonstrations at school. The administration really panicked, if you ask me. It wasn't like they were even antiwar demonstrations, though she'd told everyone that was next. She was just organizing to get some girls' athletic teams going and to relax the dress code so girls could wear slacks. Girls are still stuck in skirts and dresses, but the school had relented, sort of, on the sports. There were plans for a dance line.

Maggie was out of school now, living in a maternity home in Winona. I'd heard she'd come to the regional track meet last week. It was held in Winona, and she'd brought some of the other girls from the home with her to cheer for Red Cedar. I liked her a lot.

"How's she doing?"

"Well enough. She'll get her diploma from Winona High by the end of the summer. She doesn't plan on coming back."

I'd heard her parents wouldn't let her come back. Wouldn't let her go to the junior college, wouldn't pay tuition for any other school. She'd be on her own, now.

He took another chip. "I visit her every now and then. I don't imagine it's much spiritual help, but she likes the chance to argue about things. She had this idea, Jeff, and she said that you would be the one to help. She said that people listen to you. She must be right. I heard about today's council action." He narrowed his eyes and peered at me. "I must confess I'm a little surprised to run into you here."

He wasn't the only one. "What was her idea?"

"A phone service for teens, an emergency hot line like that Youth Emergency Service they have in the Twin Cities."

I nodded. I'd heard her talk about Y.E.S. before. At the last council meeting she'd been allowed to attend before she was removed by school officials (kicked off the council *and* the National Honor Society; pregnant girls didn't qualify), Maggie had raised the idea of the phone line. There should be some place to get answers, or just to talk, she'd pleaded.

Her round belly was already obvious when she stood up in front of those school leaders. Except for Gumbo, who sat in the back of the room shouting "Let the lady talk," most of the council booed her down.

"I could get a committee of community leaders to organize it," said Roger, "and I could get the funding. But the initial request should come from a youth, otherwise it won't happen. I think it's needed, Jeff. Would you help?"

The phone service was a good idea, even if the council members had booed it. Of course, they weren't really down on the *idea,* just the messenger. No one wanted to take a pregnant girl seriously.

"Yeah," I said softly, remembering how Maggie had looked when she'd turned and walked out of the council room. I hadn't booed, but I hadn't said anything, either. "I'd like to help."

He grabbed my hand and squeezed. "That's good. I'll be calling you. And I've got other ideas, too. I'm in town on a ten-month assignment, and I see there's a lot of work to do. I have several plans. But first, let's get this project rolling." He rose and looked around. "I should go say hello to my host."

"So you're a friend of Danny's?"

"Not really. But I did write a recommendation for him for divinity school. Mostly lies, of course, but I don't begrudge anyone the chance to avoid the draft."

"Is that why you're a minister?"

He smiled. "Not at all. I believe, I really do."

His expression made me suspicious. "In what?"

The smile disappeared. "*That* has yet to be determined."

After he danced into the crowd I left the party. I didn't feel guilty. My date was probably happier than she'd be with me. And since Tom had chosen to disappear I figured he wouldn't dare gripe about not sharing the night with his brother.

I didn't really feel like walking all the way home. I headed toward downtown, figuring I could spot someone I knew and get a ride. When I reached Main, I ducked into the book and tobacco store for some popcorn, took it out to a bench on the sidewalk, and waited for a lift home.

On a normal spring Friday night, I bet I could have flagged down a ride in two minutes, but pretty soon ten minutes passed and I still hadn't seen any friends. I decided there must be a party going on somewhere. No one had told me, not even Gumbo. Maybe it's because at the last one I'd complained about the noise, the mess, and the trouble we'd all be in if the cops knocked on the door.

"Puritan," Gumbo had snarled at me before slipping deep into an acid trip.

I'd only hung around that night to make sure he got home safely. After dropping off a few other friends, I'd finally rolled Gumbo home at about one-thirty, thinking that more and more it seemed like I was baby-sitting friends. It wasn't all that long ago that everyone was sneaking sips of scotch and gin out of the family liquor cabinet and thinking it was oh so daring. But now too many of them were doing some pretty heavy stuff. Tommy had heard rumors, and they were true.

"Evening, Jeff," someone said behind me. I looked around and nodded to Ralph Newton. He lived down the street from me and had graduated a year ago. Ralph took a final drag on a cigarette, then dropped the butt. I watched it bounce twice and roll over the curb into the gutter.

"You're dressed up. Looking for girls?" he asked.

"Looking for a ride home. You have a car?"

He nodded. "Yeah, but I'm not going that way. I'm headed to the Hi-Lo Club."

I was puzzled. Everyone knew the places in town that would serve minors. Not the Hi-Lo. Its owner was a straight law-and-order guy.

Ralph lit another cigarette and flicked the flaming match into the street. "Pudge Walton will serve me tonight. I got my induction notice. He always treats soldiers; age is no problem."

It was a warm night, but I had to shake off a sudden chill. I always cooled off and felt a knife in my stomach whenever I heard that some guy I knew got his draft notice. I hadn't even registered yet, but that didn't stop me from imagining what it felt like to get the news. Most guys weren't like my brother. Most guys I knew didn't want to be a soldier. For the ones who got the notice, it must be like hearing bad news from a doctor: You, sir, have a cancer . . . you have a disease . . . you have tested positive for war.

"I'm sorry, Ralph. Real sorry."

"Should have gone on to college, I guess. But, God, I'd waited my whole life to get out of school. Of course, it's not the end, Jeff. I've got choices. Oh, yeah, I can rip up my draft card, burn it, send the ashes to the board." I doubted it. Everyone in his family was pretty conservative. Ralph, too.

"I could go to Canada. Hell, it's closer than Chicago. And, of course, I can go to Vietnam. Bang, bang."

"Not very good choices."

"Well, there's one more. I can tell the draft board I'm queer. I'm not, but it's a way out. Think it would work? Do they have some way to check?"

"I don't know. I suppose they ask around."

"Yeah. S'pose they do." He rose, stretching. "Guess what I heard today? I heard that Sergeant Tom Ramsey's kid brother rammed a peace resolution down the throat of the high school student council. Guess that makes you a peacenik, huh, Jeff? Tell me, when it's your turn, do you plan to go to Canada?"

I couldn't speak. I had absolutely no answer.

"No, you'll be safe. Another year of high school, four of college, and by then old Nixon's secret plan for peace will have worked and we'll be out. You're absolutely safe, Jeffie. That figures — you won't have to face it, so it's cool to be against it. What does Tom think about having a peacenik for a brother? Does he like having a traitor in the family? Does he mind you spitting in his face?"

Peacenik. Well, I knew he hadn't been serious when he mentioned Canada as a choice. Not Ralph Newton.

I peered into my popcorn box and pulled out the last kernel. "We don't talk much about it."

"It's the chickens that squawk the loudest." Ralph was bobbing on his toes now and clenching his fists. I hadn't said a damn thing about the war or the draft other than to tell him I was sorry he'd gotten taken, and now all of a sudden I guessed I was about a minute away from getting punched out.

"Chickens and girls — you ever noticed that, peacenik? It's chickens and girls that mouth off against the war. Like that one who got herself knocked up. You know what I think? I think when it comes to war, girls should keep their mouths shut. Especially the sluts."

I rose and walked away. Two miles wasn't so far. I could walk. I could run. I could do anything to get out of here.

I ran across the street against the light and caused the driver of a big blue car to hit the brakes. Then came the weirdest thing: Ralph started singing. The guy had a beautiful voice that was famous in town and that had always got him the hero roles in school musicals. Now he was singing on the street corner, pointing at me while he belted out "America the Beautiful" in a clear, vibrant tenor.

I ran until I was a block away from Main, ran until the noise was muted, until I was certain I wouldn't be able to hear Ralph's singing. I stopped and listened. It was quiet, but he'd probably already headed to the Hi-Lo. Enjoy, Ralph.

The never-ending honking crescendoed, then I

heard cheering and whooping. Out of that noise rose a wild and high-pitched female voice: "Barry, no!" More honking. I looked back and saw a car pass through the intersection. It had something white looped on the antenna. Barry, whoever he was, had probably scored a bra, a favorite cruising trophy. I turned away. After fifteen minutes on Main Street I'd seen it all: packed cars cruising, boys and girls and bras, Ralph's pathos and anger. Life in the sixties, my hometown.

· 3 ·

I was startled when the phone rang. It had been the slowest night yet on the lines, and I had slipped into a reverie. In my mind I was on a big houseboat floating down the Mississippi, and close at hand was some lemonade, a good book, and a tape player reeling out Blind Faith. Perfect.

And there were no billboards. No ladders, no paint, no billboards. A week after the party where she ditched me, Tess Whippet had called up to apologize. She said she and Bobby were back together, tighter than ever, and she really owed me. Did I maybe want a job? It was the first summer in three that I hadn't planned to work at the day camp. I was seventeen, and I figured I was too old to work for no pay. So I had said no to the camp, but I hadn't lined up anything else, either. Tess's offer sounded good. Her dad owned the local billboard company, and without knowing what I was getting into, I agreed to work for minimum wage painting all of her father's billboards. Oh, not the pictures. The frames. There are several thousand billboards in southern Minnesota owned by Whippet Advertising, and their frames all needed a paint job in coffin gray. I'd been coated in it since mid-June. I never thought the day would come when I'd wake up during summer vacation and hope for bad weather, but I had begun doing just that. And of course, we'd had eight weeks of perfect summer sunshine. At least I was tan, where I wasn't gray.

It's tedious work painting billboards. Much nicer to be on a houseboat just drifting along. And that's where I was when the phone brought me back. The other two volunteers were playing gin and didn't budge from their cards. My turn.

"Y–E–S," I answered. The phones had been up and running for about six weeks, which had to have been the fastest anything ever got done anywhere. Roger Heistad — Reverend Roger, I liked to call him — was a sensational arm-twister. He could put the screws on people fast and hard and somehow make them feel good about it. He arranged all the meetings with the right people in town, and I put on the date clothes Tommy had left behind, and together Reverend Roger and I would go and make our pitch about the youth of Red Cedar needing some way to reach out in these troubled times. These are troubled times, only when you say it out loud to the kids' parents it all sounds so phony. But maybe it didn't sound that way to them because in three weeks we got the funding and the phones and the space in the back room of an empty store just off Main. I got elected to the board as a token youth, but I also volunteered to work as a phone counselor. You can go to all the planning meetings you want, but it's the real thing, the front lines, that make the difference. That's what Roger says, and I can't disagree.

Interesting guy, the Reverend. I'd been working with him on the phone project since right after we met at the party in May. He's not all that much older than my brother, but they are so unlike you'd think they were different species. He's sure not like any minister I've known before. For one thing, he doesn't wear a collar. And I've never heard him pray.

I read an article in *Life* not long ago called "The New Clergy." It was all about these young guys who go into the ministry because they love social action, not Jesus. Ministers who are more concerned with saving the world than saving souls. That's Roger all right, though he admits to faith in Christ. "Christ was an activist," he said to me once.

I don't know if Christ was an activist or not. But I like listening to Roger speculate on these things. When we're together we talk about most everything. I've probably talked more with him about the stuff I like or hate than I ever have with my brother or even Gumbo. It's nice hanging out with someone who doesn't think it's weird that I care more about world events than about the high school baseball team. I like it that *someone* takes me seriously; I've even gotten used to him calling me "Jeffrey."

I heard distant shouting from the other end of the phone. "Y–E–S," I repeated, trying to draw the caller back. "This is Heinz." We'd had to pick phone names during our training. The phone names were to keep it anonymous, but it didn't always work — not with my voice, not in this small town. Sometimes when I'd pick up the phone and speak, the caller would immediately know my voice. Then he'd pretend he had called just to see what it was all about. I always went along with that, not wanting to invade someone's privacy, not wanting to let on to some girl in my math class that I knew her boyfriend was a jerk and I knew that she was probably dying to tell someone what he was doing to her. And when the kid in my German class called I didn't dare say, Yeah, I'd wondered about those bruises. I played along and hoped they'd call again and talk to a stranger.

But if they didn't know my voice they talked, and some of the problems were so real and painful I felt sick. What could you tell anyone that would actually change things? What would help? After hearing some of the kids talk I wasn't sure I knew what to say to anyone.

Okay, I did know one thing that could help, and I had to share it pretty damn often. Thanks to Tom, I knew the easiest place to buy rubbers.

This phone call, the one that brought me all the way back from the houseboat, was for me. Not Heinz, but Jeff. I was surprised because we had another line for personal calls. It was my mom. "Jeff, that's you, isn't it? Sorry, Paul was just asking me something. Could you come home right at eleven when your shift's done?"

"Sure, Mom. Is something wrong? Do you want me now?"

"Eleven is fine."

I was a little disappointed because usually the phone volunteers would go out for coffee after working. Even when I had to be hauling paint at seven A.M. the next morning, I enjoyed the late-night talks with the others. It was a good way to unwind. I liked the people, who weren't my usual crowd of dopeheads, as Tom might say. Usually some of the other volunteers who weren't even scheduled would show up just at eleven because they knew people would be going out. Then we'd all wander over to the Country Café and order coffee or Cokes and get into everything. We'd talk about the calls we had, or books we'd read, or what was happening in the screwed-up world. Those talks were nothing special, no great revelations emerged, but they made life in a small town seem a little larger. Already I was looking forward to tomorrow's session.

Paul was sitting on the step when I walked up the sidewalk. All the lights were on, and I could see several people milling around in the living room. "It's a work night, isn't it?" I asked. "Are you guys having a party?"

I liked Paul. Since the night Tom stood naked in the kitchen he and Mom had been pretty steady, and that was nice because she was home more on weekends and drinking less. I sure didn't mind cooking for an extra person.

He rose and put his arms around me and squeezed hard. "Your brother . . ." He couldn't finish the sentence. He didn't need to. No one who had a brother serving in Vietnam in 1969 needed to hear the rest of that sentence.

Tom was dead. Beautiful, star-blessed, lovable, happy Tom had shipped out from Pendleton and lasted six weeks in Vietnam.

I went into the house and found my mother. She was on the phone, evidently trying to track down my dad. I took her hand and looked at her. Not a trace of tears. She tossed a box of Kleenex to Danny Miller, who was crying to beat the band at the kitchen table. Word must have spread fast because there was a crowd in the house, all of them milling aimlessly, drinking coffee or booze, crying, or telling stories about Tom and laughing.

"Yes, of course, I'll wait," Mom said into the phone. She kept it pressed to her ear, but swung the mouthpiece up. She turned to me. "At two o'clock today, Paul walks across the floor of the plant, big grin on his face, and what do you know but he asks me to marry him. As soon as work gets out we take off for Rochester because he wants to buy me a ring at Hudson's and celebrate with steaks at Michael's."

Everyone was crowded around us now, listening.

"We had a great time at the jewelry store, checking out every rock they've got. And this clerk kept following us around because obviously we weren't the usual Mayo doctor customer they get, but I tell you, Paul's money fit just fine into their till."

I took her left hand and rubbed across the bare fingers. "Where is it?"

"Getting sized. I have very bony fingers, you know. Oh, we were having fun, Jeffie, and we had no idea that all that time they were waiting for us. Where were you after work?"

"I met Gumbo at the pool, then went straight to the phones."

She nodded and scratched at a spot of dried paint on my pants. "That's what I figured. When we got home at nine the doorbell rang before I'd even poured a drink. Right then I had never been happier in my life. I opened the door, and as soon as I saw these two soldiers, well, I knew. Then I heard this voice that could have come out of a robot telling me that Tommy is dead. 'Written confirmation, Ma'am, will follow.' That's what the SOB said." She cranked the phone mouthpiece back into position. "Yeah, I'm still here. No? Well, when he does, tell him his ex-wife called and I want to hear from him tomorrow. Yeah, you, too, honey," she spat into the phone.

My mom's hair color was naturally a dull brown, which she often altered with various colored rinses. Lately, she had been trying reds, and now it was the color of strong tea. It sort of looked like she had ducked her head into a pail of Lipton. I pushed a strand of her tea-colored hair behind her ear and caressed her cheek with my finger. There was a whole roomful of people watching us. Just what did they want?

"Well," I said, "it's good news about you and Paul."

The cigarette in her hand was having a shaky trip to

her mouth. She glanced at me, and our identical blue eyes were a mirror image of pain and wonder. "Oh, yeah," she whispered. "Ain't it, though?"

I hugged her. The cigarette fell. I was drained and numb, but I could feel her rumbling all the way through. Her face was pressed against my chest, and her shoulders were in my arms. The rumbling was deep, but climbing, and I could feel it building, rising, clawing its way up, stronger and harder until she was shaking. Then the howl emerged: "Tommy!"

It takes over a week to get a body back from Vietnam, and then it arrives with an escort. I never knew that there are actually Marines whose job it is to travel with bodies and stay with the families of the dead soldiers until after the funeral. Some job.

The escort staying with us was a sergeant, a career guy named O'Keefe. He was a rigid, big-chested guy who slept in my room right across from the peace poster and never said a thing. Never said much about anything. I couldn't figure out why he was here. Couldn't figure out why the military went to the trouble and expense of sending out guys with every body. Every body. That's about ninety, one hundred each week. At least. I read somewhere they're predicting ten thousand dead this year. And that's just on our side.

"How often do you do this?" I was fixing the sarge coffee. He drank a lot of it. The sun hadn't been up long and already he was in full, sharp-pressed uniform. I was in shorts, not sharp-pressed.

"As often as needed. It's full-time until I get new orders." He tasted his coffee and gave a quick nod of satisfaction. I'd observed that that was how the sarge moved: precise, exact, nothing wasted. Not like my brother, not like wild, dancing, arms-flailing, legs-churning Tommy.

I poured my own coffee, sipped, spat it out. Too hot; now my tongue would be touchy all day. "Doesn't it get to you, all these families?"

"No, sir."

That was probably true enough. In the twenty-four hours he'd been with us he had proven to be a very still and gracious figure in the middle of nonstop craziness. The moment word had gotten out of Tom's death people had started coming over, and I don't think anyone had gone home, except maybe Paul, who went to his apartment every night and returned the next morning with fresh flowers for Mom. None of it touched the sarge: not my mother's frequent collapses into tears and howling or her tirade when my father called to say, Sorry, but I can't come to the funeral; not the stream of friends with food and cases of beer; not Reverend Roger's loud antiwar ministrations, which had caused one or two other people to fight until Paul stepped in; not even Gumbo's twelve-hour motionless nap on the sofa.

I eyed the sarge over my cup. I wanted to see him wince, wanted to see him show some feeling. Wanted him to sit in his shorts on the sofa, knock back a few beers, and speak honestly to the brother and mother of dead body number . . . what would it be, 25? 125? 525?

Speak to us, Sergeant, and tell us what it looks like in the jungle where Tommy died. You've been there. Tell us about the smell of blood and the sounds of guns. Which is louder, an M–16 or a screaming, wounded soldier?

Just tell us.

He shifted. "It's an honor to do this. These soldiers are heroes."

That was exactly what I didn't want to hear because I couldn't believe it. Couldn't believe that they were heroes, when I knew that most of them were unwilling soldiers, just trapped boys with nowhere to go. Boys like Ralph Newton, whose number had finally come up and they had no way to get around it. Don't call them heroes, Sarge, not when they're really only guys trapped at a dead end.

I poured out my coffee. Time to get dressed for the burial. "These soldiers may be heroes," I said, "but these soldiers are dead."

Mom had decided to have no formal service, just a few words at the gravesite. Quite a crowd had come to the cemetery, and I stood straight and tall in my brother's very best date clothes. I guess they weren't borrowed anymore. They were mine, now.

My mother had asked Roger to say a few words. Say anything, she'd ordered. Anything at all.

For once Roger was stingy with words. He led everyone in the Twenty-third Psalm, then blessed the coffin, closed his eyes, and spoke firmly: "God Almighty, this must stop."

They folded the flag then. Sarge was assisted by a staff officer from the local recruiting office, and the two of them sure as hell knew how to fold a flag. Coffins are big, and flags made to cover them are even bigger. Tom's flag was as big as the blanket on a giant's bed, but those two soldiers had it folded into a taut and tidy triangle in maybe forty-five seconds. Sarge handed it to Mom. A keepsake, Ma'am. Wipe your tears with this.

The sarge split as soon as we returned to the house. His job was done; he'd brought home the hero. I followed him out to his government car. What does one say? Thanks for the delivery? "Um, thanks," I muttered, the best I could do.

He was the one with the words. "I liked that minister: 'God Almighty, this must stop.' I pray for that every day, Jeff. And I pray for all my families. You take care now." He saluted and got into his car.

The ten-day open house continued for a few hours longer. A few more hours of food and tears and stories. About midnight Paul chased everyone out, which maybe was a mistake because the house was suddenly too quiet. One of the three of us couldn't even breathe without someone else turning around and asking, What did you say? Then Paul went home, and it was just Mom and me. It was the first time we'd been alone together since we found out Tommy was dead.

We looked at each other.

Finally: "Hell of a day," she said.

"Oh, yeah," I answered.

"I think," she said, "that I'll go back to work tomorrow."

"I probably will, too."

"Oh, you should know, the other day Paul and I were coming back from Kremer's Liquors and we saw a billboard that was in real bad shape."

"Where?"

"On Oakland, about Third Street Northeast."

"I've mostly been doing rural signs."

"Oh, sure. Well, I told you. Good night, honey."

"Night, Mom."

My brother's funeral day, and that's how we said good night, by saying good night. Night, Mom.

I stripped down to my briefs and crawled into bed. I pulled the sheet up over my head, and it was all so still and dark. Not a sound, not a glimmer of light.

Still and dark, like a body bag, like a coffin.

Tommy. Others. Tommy.

God Almighty. This must stop.

· 4 ·

NBC shows the most bodies. I don't know who its cameraman is, but he must be incredibly gutsy because he's always got his lens right in the faces of the wounded. There seems to be sort of a protocol about showing wounded and dead guys: close-ups of living anguish are okay, but take ten steps back for the dead.

There was a shot last week on CBS of soldiers loading body bags. I don't know how they got away with it. The Pentagon must hate it when that sort of thing gets out — pictures of rows and rows of bags getting loaded for transport back to the States. Pretty grim. It set me to thinking about all the history classes I've had over the years. History is always one of two things, religion or war, and sometimes of course they're one and the same. But in all those years of studying history, never once did I read in a book or hear from a teacher anything about the simple things, like, How did they ship the bodies home?

This is the kind of stuff I want to know now, and when I ask I get in trouble. Henry Dutton, who has to be the world's most boring teacher, nearly had a fit last week when I raised my hand and interrupted his lecture on sonnets. Sonnets are okay. Very orderly and pretty. What I wanted to know was how much a book of sonnets would have cost someone back in, say, 1830. Everyone laughed, and Dutton chuckled and tried to go on. I asked again, and that peeved him. But my questions were important. Who could buy the stupid sonnets? Were they printed in newspapers? In books? Read aloud in a park and then tacked to the door of a tavern?

I don't mind learning about dead poets and their fourteen-line poems, but if they weren't important to the people back then, why should they be important to me?

So I kept raising my hand to get an answer, and he kept ignoring me. He could have just said, I don't know the answer, Jeff. I've never heard a teacher say that, though. Dutton simply pretended the question wasn't being asked. Pretended until he couldn't continue to ignore me, then he wheeled around from where he was diagramming the poem on the blackboard and said, Perhaps I should ask my questions in the office.

The same thing happened in history class on Monday. We were discussing the Napoleonic Wars. I raised my hand to ask a question. Just to ask, not to irritate, not like the time Gumbo kept bugging Mrs. Shaw about military armor and did she know how soldiers wearing chain mail went to the bathroom? He didn't really care, he was just trying to embarrass her. But I had questions that needed answers. We were talking about these huge wars that engulfed Europe, and I wanted to know who the soldiers were. Had they been drafted? Were they peasants? Rich boys? How much were they paid? Who fought Napoleon's wars for him, Mrs. Shaw? Did anyone ask them if they wanted to die?

She tried to roll right over it. Couldn't admit she didn't know. Just disregard the boy and roll on to the next map. I kept raising my hand, then speaking out when she ignored me.

How old were the youngest soldiers?

Did they get mail from their mothers?

Please, Mrs. Shaw, how were the bodies shipped home?

She finally whirled around from the blackboard, chalk dust flying up, and she pointed to the door. "To the office, Jeff Ramsey."

I didn't bother with the office. Not that I expected anything awful. The principal, Mr. Spicer, was always fairer than fair. I knew he'd just ask me if I had brought anything to study, then point me to a chair. I've made maybe fourteen trips to the office this fall, and that's all he's ever done.

People make allowances for the dead soldier's brother.

I didn't want to bother Mr. Spicer. So after Mrs. Shaw sent me packing, I just walked past the class-rooms, down the hall, through the wide doors, and went straight on home. I've been here since.

I guess I've gone AWOL.

I can get away with it because Mom and Paul are

still in Vegas on their honeymoon. The school secretary calls every day, and I've just told her I'm sick. What can they do?

Absent-with-out-leave.

Gumbo brought me some homework, and one of the other Y.E.S. volunteers, Andrea, brought over some carry-out food from the Country Café. Last night she walked right in and caught me standing on the kitchen table in my underwear. I was holding a cap full of golf balls. It's sort of a project I've been working on, but I didn't try to explain and she didn't ask. I could tell that I freaked her out, and I bet she won't bring me any more food. And I've fought with Gumbo, so he probably won't bring me any more assignments. Which is okay because I haven't been doing the work. I'm still a student, though. A student of television.

Gumbo came by yesterday right at news time, and I had to keep telling him to hush during the footage from Vietnam. He was just chatting on and on while they showed this film of a village getting hit by U.S. bombers. He was talking so much that I didn't even hear if the village was in the north or the south. I finally told him to shut the hell up or get out. He screamed at me then and wanted to know why every time he came over I was glued to the set watching the war. I headed him to the door then and told him if he didn't like it he should come over later and we'd watch "The Beverly Hillbillies." That was the fight.

I do watch a lot of news. National, local, anything. This week alone there were two special reports from the war. I watch because I want to see a guy get killed. I want to see a young soldier walk straight into a bullet or get tossed up in an explosion. They haven't shown anything like that yet. I'm waiting. The letter Mom got from the Marines said Tom died instantly as a result of sniper fire. I want to see sniper fire. I want to see what happened.

Mostly it's bombing. This past week the U.S. and the South Vietnamese have cleaned out and burned three villages in the south while the bombers took care of a few more in the north. Relocating the population, the official reports put it. I wonder how much fire-power it takes to relocate the population of a single village. Probably about half as much as is actually used.

I've been relocating my own populations. The other night I blew a fuse when I plugged in the popcorn popper while the toaster was going. When I went down to the basement to fix the fuse I saw a lot of old toys Mom had put away. There was a giant box of Legos I used to play with when I was a kid. I hauled it off the shelf and took it upstairs. Legos are the perfect toy. I don't know why I ever stopped playing with them.

I started building villages. Red and blue and yellow villages. Little conclaves of huts and shops and temples, all in primary colors. Then I wrecked them.

It took me a while to figure out an effective weapon. Legos lock together tightly, and they resisted most of the things I found. Until I remembered Tommy's golf balls.

That's what I was doing when Andrea walked in on me. She said she had rung the bell and knocked and then walked in and called my name. I didn't hear her. That's how she happened to find me in the kitchen in my underwear. I just hadn't bothered getting dressed yesterday. At least I was wearing boxers, which probably covered more than my swimsuit. Still, she was a little upset, and she got out fast.

Too bad, because she missed a good show. It was the first time I'd figured out how to use the golf balls, and they worked really well. The Legos went flying apart. Red, yellow, and blue bricks everywhere. There are probably some little ones under the fridge that I'll never get out.

I spent this afternoon rebuilding the village, and it's all ready for another attempt at population relocation. This should be even better because tonight I've got more firepower. I've added steelies to the golf balls. They're from Tommy's old marble collection. He used to beat me up for getting into it. Not now. Like his car and his clothes, I guess his marbles are mine now.

The Lego village covers about three square feet on the kitchen floor. I'm six-foot-one, and the table is three feet high, so that puts me over nine feet above the village. I don't know if that's accurate scale. I have no idea how high the bombers fly. Maybe closer? Or are they so high they can't be seen? What do they sound like? I wonder if the villagers hear them before they see them. Or is the explosion the first sign that the good ol' U.S.A. has come to visit?

The steelies added a lot of weight to the cap. Dead weight, which is good because the golf balls bounce on impact. Last night one of them hit the oven door and left a dent.

It's tempting to aim and drop the ammo one at a time, but that's not the way the U.S. military bombs a village. Nope, the whole payload has to go at once. Ready . . . aim . . .

"Mother of Christ, what are you doing, Jeffrey?"

I steadied the cap and looked behind me. "Hey there, Reverend Roger. You should watch your language. And knock next time. Man, no one knocks anymore."

He walked into the kitchen. "I knocked. You just didn't hear. What are you doing?" He toed the Lego structure. "And what's this?"

"A Vietnamese village. You're just in time for the bombing. Come up here and watch."

He joined me without even thinking about it. I guess ministers are used to playing along. I handed him the cap. "You do the honors."

He bounced the payload in his hands, and the steelies knocked together. Then he tipped it over. In an instant there was an explosion of colored bricks, steel marbles, and golf balls. Roger cringed and turned away just as a golf ball bounced back and hit him on the rump.

We surveyed the damage in silence. This was just play, but it still felt awful. It could all be picked up, of course, and there were no bodies to bury. That was the difference.

I felt Roger's hand on my shoulder. "Go get dressed," he said.

By the time I returned he had all the Legos on the table and he was sorting them by color into the different compartments in their box. He was sipping a soda and humming as he separated the little bricks. He pointed to a chair. "Sit down and listen."

I got my own soda first, and I took a long time opening it and filling a glass with ice. Roger waited without saying a word.

Finally, I sat down. I smiled at the pastor. "How 'bout those Vikings?"

No jokes. He was definitely not here to joke.

"Andrea and Gumbo have both called me," he said. "Andrea was especially upset. She said she came over last night and she found you like . . . like you were, Jeffrey. And it scared her. Gumbo told me that you haven't been in school all week."

"There's no reason to go to school, Roger. They can't answer my questions. They don't teach anything worthwhile. There's nothing to learn."

He slammed his fist on the table. "Of course there isn't, but that's not the point of high school!" He covered his forehead with his hand and started massaging his temple. I wondered if I should offer him something stronger than soda, something from Mom's bottom cupboard. He looked up abruptly and slapped his hands together. "Dammit, Jeffrey, it's not just that you've been skipping school. For weeks you have been hiding. Andrea said you haven't worked the phones all fall. She said that you're the best trainer and without you the new volunteers are having a miserable time."

"She exaggerates."

"I haven't seen you at a Y.E.S. board meeting since summer. I let it pass because I knew things have been rough. But I didn't know they were this bad." His hand made a sweeping motion through the air.

"Do you know why I can't work on the phones, Roger? Because I can't help. I can't give anyone advice. It would be hypocritical. I don't know anything that would help anyone, and I won't pretend that I do. That's your game, Reverend."

I wished I hadn't said it. The jab hit home, hard and sharp. Roger paled, and he nodded. He looked so tense, so wound up. He rubbed the back of his neck. I wanted to reach across and do it for him, the way I massage my mom at night when she's wired from eight hours of tedious plant work. But it would seem weird to touch a guy that way, so I kept my hand to myself.

He picked up a golf ball and bounced it. "Have you ever cracked one of these open? Inside it's like a long rubber band wrapped around a hard tiny core."

I got a meat mallet out of a drawer and brought it back to the table. We sat on the floor and took turns hammering the golf ball until it split open. Roger began unraveling the rubber. "Do you golf?" he asked.

"Never tried it. They were Tom's. He loved to golf. Loved to play anything. You never met him, did you, Roger?"

"Yes I did. At that party where I met you."

"That's right. Tom loved parties. He loved being with people."

"From all that I've heard, people loved being with him. Evidently he was a very popular fellow."

"He was. His friends still like to come around the house, just to be here and talk. It's hard on Mom, but she sort of likes it, too."

He tossed me the nearly eviscerated golf ball. "Your turn. When do they get back from the honeymoon?"

"Sunday."

"That was the sweetest wedding I've ever done. And the first one that wasn't in a church."

"She wouldn't do that. She wouldn't even have had a minister, except for you."

He looked around the kitchen. "How many people were here? Fifty? Sixty?"

"Eighty-seven."

He whistled. "I thought it was crowded."

I finished unraveling the rubber and held up the tiny metal core. I rolled it between my fingers, then dropped it on the floor. We watched as it bounced once, then rolled across the floor and disappeared under the stove. "That's where half my Lego collection is," I said. "Or under the fridge."

Roger wasn't listening to me. "This damn war," he muttered.

"Well, yeah. What else is new?"

"Have you ever thought how many more casualties of war there are beyond the official numbers?"

"Do you mean the Vietcong dead? They add those up, Roger. They brag about the numbers, in fact."

He shook his head. "No, I mean like you. Others. Lives changed and destroyed." He shrugged. "Like me. Did I ever tell you that my father hasn't talked to me in two years? The first time I spoke out against the war was in an editorial in the seminary paper. He read it and ever since has refused to speak to me. If I call home and he answers instead of my mother, he just hangs up without a word. He was an army major in World War II. He lost an arm. My mother says he believes I'm dishonoring him by opposing the war." He rose, picked up the rubber remnants and the ball shell, and deposited them in the trash. He stood at the sink to wash his hands. "Will you do me a favor, Jeffrey?"

"If I can, Roger."

He turned from the sink, looked about for a towel, then whipped his hands in the air to dry them. "Two favors. First, go back to school. Grit your teeth and straighten up — go back, and be the good and useful boy that everyone expects Jeff Ramsey to be. Not for me, not for you, not for the phone service. Do it for your mother. She's already lost one boy. Don't make it two. Don't go crazy on her."

"She hasn't lost two boys. I haven't freaked out, Roger. I haven't gone over the edge, okay? She hasn't lost me."

"She might not see the difference."

"There is a difference. I'm just taking some time off. I needed to step out for a while."

"It's time to step back in. People need you. Your mother does."

"Could we talk about the second favor?"

"Next Wednesday I'm going up to Minneapolis for the moratorium demonstration at the U. of M. Come with me."

"You just asked me to go back to school. Wednesday's a school day. I'd have to skip."

"For a good reason, not just because you want to hide out at home in your underwear and play with Legos."

I shook my head. I'd been reading about plans for the moratorium for weeks. All across the country on the same day there would be mass demonstrations against the war. "I don't see the point. Nixon's not going to be persuaded to stop the war. If anything, he'll just heat it up."

"It's important to speak out. And it's important that the people in this town know that Tom Ramsey's brother is against the war. That's where it will make a difference."

I couldn't believe that. I couldn't believe that by adding my one voice to the thousands there would be any difference. I couldn't believe that by going and being one more warm body in a mob I would change anything.

I knew Roger wouldn't be persuaded by an argument of political futility. After all, the very first time I met him he told me he was a believer. I'd have to try something else. "I'm not sure Mom would feel good about it."

He raised his hands in disbelief. "Jeffrey! You skip school and spend a week in your underwear and then say that she might not like you taking a field trip with a minister?"

Roger always was a sensational arm-twister. He could argue with God and win.

I shrugged. "Will you buy me breakfast that day?"

"Breakfast, lunch, air fare to Jamaica — I'll buy. Just come."

I promised, and he was happy.

I was careful to lock all the doors after Roger was gone; I didn't want anyone else walking in on me. I fixed a bowl of cereal and flipped on the television. The local late news often had network footage from the war. Tonight it was the same film ABC had run at five-thirty — villages and bombers. The anchor kept tripping over the Vietnamese words, mutilating the names of hamlets and officials. I could have done better.

I would never renege, but already I regretted my promise to Roger. Why march and protest? Why bother with all the chants, all the slogans, all the speeches and songs? The dead would remain dead, with more to join them every day.

· 5 ·

In spite of my promise to Roger, I didn't go back to school until Monday. Mom and Paul returned Sunday night, and I swear two minutes hadn't passed before Mom looked at me suspiciously and asked, What had been going on around here? I told her, Nothing, only I'd been sort of sick and I stayed home and she'd have to write a note. Sick? she wanted to know, but turned away before she got an answer she wouldn't like.

She wrote me the note, and then one again yesterday to excuse me for today because I was going up to Minneapolis to take part in a political protest. I think I am probably the first person in the history of Red Cedar Senior High to get excused for a peace rally.

Paul was in the shower, Mom was in her bathrobe, and I was in Tom's date clothes when Roger arrived at five-thirty A.M. It was drizzling, and Mom forced a raincoat on me before following me out to the driveway. Roger, always the gentleman, sprang out of the car when he spotted her.

I happen to know that my mother doesn't wear much in the way of pajamas. Actually, she wears nothing at all. I only know this because two days before the wedding some of her girlfriends were over for what turned into an all-night party, and when I started cleaning the kitchen at midnight they were just deciding to make it a sleepover. Mom told them that they'd have to improvise with pajamas because she didn't use them and didn't have any. I ended up supplying the women with T-shirts.

So I knew that she probably didn't have anything on under the robe, and she was having a hard time keeping it closed while she lit a cigarette and talked with Roger. I suppose she wouldn't blink about revealing something of herself at dawn. It was Roger I was worried about.

I stepped between them. "Go get dressed, Mom. You're due at work in thirty minutes."

"I married the boss. A few minutes won't matter." She reached into her robe pocket and withdrew a little box. "You wear this today, Jeff. You wear it and go yell with the others. Make so much noise that Tricky Dick can't ignore it."

"You could join us," said Roger.

"If it weren't for Paul's brother, I just might. He's a lifer in the Navy, Roger. He's an honorable man, and he's so hurt by all the protests."

I could tell Roger was stringing together the words to argue with her, so I turned him around and put him back into the car. Mom followed me to deliver a kiss, then ran back to the house.

We were a good ten miles out of town and at least three minutes into one of Roger's political monologues when I remembered to look in the box Mom had slipped into my pocket. I shifted my weight onto my left hip and dug after the box.

Wear it and yell, she'd said. I opened the box. Lying on a soft, white cotton square was her Gold Star pin, the tiny medal of honor given to every mother of a dead soldier.

I wonder how the police estimate the size of crowds. Do they have some formula based on square footage or something? I bet it's less scientific. I bet it's all done with a shrug and a guess, sort of the way Paul spices chili: "What the hell, why don't we add a little bit more?"

The crowd on the U. of M. mall was too big for me to guess the size. Thousands, and every face different. Mostly students, of course, but plenty of older people. And lots of women. When we first reached the mall there was this old lady standing on some steps. She was kind of dancing, and the people around her were going wild. She got everyone worked up in a chant. I could see my mom like that in a few years, if only she'd quit messing with her hair and let it go natural. I could see her, gray and loud, getting people to have a better time than they'd planned on.

I could have watched the woman for a long time, but Roger suddenly shrieked. He yanked me on the arm and charged us both through the crowd.

"Morris," he howled. "Hi-dee-ho, Morris!" People turned toward the yelling, and they must have had an eyeful: a short, round, balding guy towing a six-foot telephone pole. And the worst thing was we were both dressed the same. In honor of my first trip to the campus, I'd gotten my hair cut and even ironed my clothes. By unhappy accident, Roger had also worn a blue shirt and tan pants. We looked like two thirds of a folk music trio.

A tall, bearded man several hundred people away responded to Roger's howling with a yelp and his own charge through the crowd. The two men met in a hug, then launched into a nonstop exchange of gossip that was overheard by hundreds of people but involved none of them.

Guess who's been called by a church in Alabama, said Morris.

I heard Whitman and that girl split, said Roger.

The deacon . . . offered Morris.

When I move to Georgia . . . said Roger.

New churches. Old courses. A vacation in Bermuda. Lovers and friends and do you still have that old Dodge?

Finally: "You'll meet her at Wendell's later," said Morris. "You'll come for dinner, won't you?"

"Of course," boomed Roger.

I had to protest. This rally, if it didn't get going soon, would take the whole day. I hadn't told Mom anything about getting back late, and, after all, I had lots of schoolwork to make up. I tugged on Roger's arm. "We're not staying, are we?"

He nodded vigorously. "We must. Morris has come up all the way from Davenport. And you should meet his brother Wendell. He's a visionary, Jeff. A true visionary." Roger then introduced me to Morris, who shook my hand heartily as he said something about growing up next door to Roger in Keokuk. Then Roger had to unzip his mouth and say I was making an important statement by coming today because I was the brother of a Marine killed in action. He lifted a single eyebrow and tapped the little gold star I'd pinned to my shirt.

Morris grabbed my hand again, looked at the pin, then stared into my eyes. "Beautiful," he said.

Not really, I wanted to say, but his earnestness silenced me.

"Morris's brother just got some Ford Foundation money to study the root causes of ghetto violence."

"Does your brother know a lot about ghettos?" I asked.

"He's an expert."

An expert who grew up in Keokuk. This interested me and I wanted to ask about it, but just then Roger tugged on my arm. "That's the building, Jeffrey. That's the physics building they tried to blow up last summer. That's the one."

Morris swore and said something about freaks setting the movement back ten years. A man in front of us twirled around, anger oozing out of his eyes, and grunted, "Not stupid at all. If the authorities can wage their wars with bombs, then so can we!"

Morris shoved his face within inches of the stranger's. "And just how good a job of winning the war have those bombs been doing?"

102

I really thought they were going to slug it out. Blows and blood. Peace, man.

Roger stepped in. "This is a day of unity," he said as he placed a hand on each man's chest. "Nothing but unity will solve any problems, including the war. Please, gentlemen, let's not fight with each other."

The preacher's homily worked. Morris crossed his arms and looked away. The bomb-approving stranger turned and walked off.

I grinned at Roger. "If they were any younger," I whispered to him, "you could have spanked them."

He smiled wanly. "Younger and smaller."

I looked at the building that had generated the argument. The bombing had been big news for a few days last summer. One girl had stayed behind and died. I hadn't paid much attention because it all happened right about the time of Tom's funeral.

I didn't see that the building was anything to fight over. It was only a handsome pile of bricks. Just one more place where one more person had died.

Something must have started up front because suddenly the crowd surged forward a few steps. I stumbled into a woman. She turned around, smiled, and handed me a button. It was black with bold letters: *Stop School, Stop Work, Stop War.* I thanked her and pinned it below the star. The crowd crushed again, then settled.

Even though we had arrived early, thousands had come before us and we were too far from the speakers' stand to hear anything. People were jammed together on the lawns, the sidewalks, the footbridges over the street. My height was definitely an advantage, and I used it to watch people. There were hippies and straights, old and young, blacks and whites. Unity. If that's what was needed to get anything done, then this crowd could do it. I hoped Roger was right.

After an hour of speeches that I couldn't hear, there was a loud cheer that soon evolved into a deep chant: Out Now! Out Now! Then we were moving.

I was glad to be walking. The crowd poured onto the wide street and turned toward the downtown area. Two miles ahead of us I could see the city's lone skyscraper, the IDS Building. At fifty stories, it was nearly twice as tall as any other building in the city, and it stood like a defiant middle finger rising out of a knuckled skyline. Exactly my mood.

I'd never before walked in the middle of the city. And once the marchers crossed the bridge over the Mississippi River and passed a few campus buildings, we were definitely in the city. It was a picture meant for black-and-white film: trash dumped in vacant lots, empty stores, dark taverns with dirty glass fronts that revealed lines of men bellied up to the bar at eleven A.M.

Roger was talking to everyone around us. I envied his love of a crowd and the almost sensual pleasure he seemed to get out of human interaction. I heard him tell several people that I was a Gold Star brother. I shrugged off his encouragement to join any of the debates and discussions going on around us. I was here to march.

We turned when the Mississippi did, and the march followed the river upstream. I could see the cluster of flour mills along the banks. The mills were the businesses that had brought settlers and power and money, and that had created the city.

I was a meatpacker's kid from a town in southern Minnesota, and I wouldn't know power and money if someone dropped it on me from the top of the IDS tower. But I knew this much: power and money made wars, and power and money could stop them. We were headed to the power and money center of the largest city in my home state. Suddenly I was ready to yell, to chant, to sing and shout. Out Now!

By the time we arrived at the Federal Building the crowd had grown to maybe twice the size it had been at the university. There were plenty of people in suits. I could see a line of counterprotesters across the street. They were shouting and jeering and brandishing signs. I nudged Roger and pointed to one hand-lettered poster: PRO-RED PREACHERS ARE PHONIES. Roger shrugged. "I've seen and heard worse," he said calmly.

I was sure he had. Maybe from his own father. A wave of affection warmed me, and I hugged him. Roger looked surprised. "Thanks for making me come," I said.

He was prevented from responding when a roar went up. Someone had come out of the Federal Building and lowered the flag to half-mast. It was a good sign. Not everyone with power or money opposed us.

We were close enough this time actually to hear the

speakers. A congressman spoke, and he was simultaneously booed and cheered. Two poets read their poems, neither of which I could follow, but all around me other people were getting both teary and aroused. The poets received wild ovations.

The speeches and the breaks between speeches dragged on. By the time some ministers began a requiem for the war dead, the crowd was pretty restless and many people were departing. No one around us went forward to take the bread and wine being distributed as part of the service. As the businessmen and students and grandmas and grandpas departed, a few people up front, evidently organizers, waved arms in an attempt to get everyone to stay for the service. They shouldn't have bothered. It was past lunchtime, and a light rain was falling; there was no way this crowd would hang around.

"Now that we're done here," I said to Roger and Morris, "maybe someone should check and see if they stopped the war." Morris smiled, but Roger jabbed a finger against my chest.

"Damn your cynicism, Jeffrey," he said, "You are seventeen, and you have not earned that cynicism."

Roger's finger packed a wallop. I stepped back. "I apologize, Reverend. It's been a wonderful day."

Morris grunted and looked up at the sky. Raindrops trailed off his ear. "This wonderful day is a bit on the wet side. Let's get out of it. I know a good place to have lunch before we catch a bus back to Wendell's."

"Not me," I said.

"What?" asked Roger.

"I want to walk back. I'll get my own lunch and meet you later. You don't want me around for your reunion. Just give me Wendell's address, and I'll meet you there later. Don't look at me like that, Roger."

Morris was already scribbling on the back of a deposit slip from his checkbook. "It's only two blocks from campus. Anyone can give you directions. And if you get tired of walking, any number sixteen bus will take you back."

Roger puffed his cheeks and shook his head. "Absolutely not. I'm responsible —"

"Yes, you are, Reverend Roger," I said as I took the paper from Morris and shoved it into a pocket. "You are very responsible. People like that about you." I fastened the top snap of my rain slicker. "I'll be there by supper."

I retraced the route we'd taken from the university. The rain had convinced most people to catch a bus, so I pretty much had the sidewalks to myself. Minneapolis is supposed to be a beautiful city, with something like a dozen lakes and a string of parks. Not in this neighborhood. The street was littered with trash dropped by the marchers, and the sidewalks glittered with the broken glass of bottles. I cut over two blocks to the riverfront, hoping to catch some green and find a park bench to sit on. Even in the rain, a little sit-down would have been welcome. After three hours of nonstop voices, I needed a quiet place.

The Mississippi River is one of the largest and longest rivers in the world. I'd spent a lot of time on it because Gumbo's grandpa has a cabin on the river just north of Wabasha and I'd always been invited along when his family visited. I learned to swim and water-ski there. Some days Gumbo and I would beachcomb for hours, collecting agates or driftwood that was so smoothed by the water that it seemed alien and alive. Or we'd climb back in the rocky bluffs, watching for rattlesnakes, and picnic on a spot overlooking the water. There's some beer company from around there that calls the Mississippi Valley God's Country. I won't argue with that.

But right here in Minneapolis they've turned the Mighty Miss into nothing more than a concrete storm and sewer runoff. The street I was on dead-ended at a high wall that blocked any view of the river. No access, no riverbanks, no benches. The river was walled in, dammed up, and unapproachable. I could see the towers of the mills, but I couldn't see the water that fueled them.

Power and money, again. Men used them to strangle the world's greatest river. And the kind of thinking that says we can do that, I realized, was the kind of thinking that says it's okay to bomb a little country in order to free it. I kicked an empty glass bottle. It flew up, hit the wall, and shattered.

It started pouring and I hustled back to Washington Avenue, where I hailed a bus just as it began to pull away from the curb. I questioned the driver about the fare, and he smiled and answered, adding a question: "Freshman, huh?" I dropped the coins into the box and found a seat without speaking.

The bus slowed down on the bridge over the river. Through the curtain of rain I could see that at this spot the city loosened its grip on the Mississippi. Trees actually grew on the banks and concrete embankments gave way to rocks and spotty beaches. The river was free of the city. Wet and cold, stuffed with speeches and arguments, I wanted that, too.

There was a crowd in the apartment when I finally found my way to the address Morris had given me. The sky had cleared and I'd spent time wandering around the university. Then I'd spent a little more time in the record shops just off campus. I bought Gumbo two new releases that he'd never be able to find in Red Cedar, and those purchases cheered me. I'd go home with something other than a picture of the tamed and dirty river.

I was planning on asking to play the albums when I got to the apartment, but as soon as a woman opened the door and motioned me into the crowd I gave up that idea. There was no music in this place.

Roger waved and made his way to me. "I was worried," he said. "I should never have let you go."

I nodded to Morris, who hallooed from a davenport, where he was sitting with three women. One had her hands in his hair. Roger took the albums and peeled the slicker off me. He disappeared with them down a hall, then returned looking wildly happy. "Wonderful things, Jeffrey. Just wonderful things being said here. These are the people who are absolutely in the middle of a revolution. They're making things happen. Come, you must meet Wendell."

He ushered me to a man about his own age who was throned in an overstuffed chair. People were actually sitting at his feet. I took a good look because I'd never seen a visionary before.

Wendell acknowledged our introduction by rising and hugging me. He offered me a joint. I refused it. "Roger," he said in a long, smoky exhalation, "has told us all about you, Jeffrey. Welcome to my home."

Someone else demanded his attention then, so I stepped aside. Roger had been absorbed into a nearby argument, and it appeared I was on my own. I stood by a bookcase and tried to amuse myself by studying the titles while eavesdropping on all the conversations. I had talked with Roger often about the people he'd known from college or seminary who had truly risked health and life by serving in the Peace Corps or registering voters in the south. Morris, who now had a hash pipe in his mouth, had even been jailed in Mississippi. I didn't doubt that they and others were driven by a desire to stand up to any injustice. I had heard and read stories, and I believed them.

But today it seemed as if pot and wine and talk seemed to be the stuff that drove these people. The talk bored me. The smoke irritated my eyes. I wanted a glass of cold water.

A baby was bouncing in a spring-hung contraption in the doorway to the kitchen. He looked up at me as I eased around him.

A woman stood at the sink, leaning on her arms over the porcelain. Tears streamed down her cheeks.

Before I could back out, she turned and smiled. "Don't panic," she said. "It's the onions."

"Happens to my mother," I said. "I don't get so bothered. Could I help you?"

"What?"

"Could I help you?"

"What's your name?"

"Jeff Ramsey. I'm visiting —"

"Jeff, would you marry me?"

I wondered if onions could drive you wacko. Or maybe it was the influence of the wine in the bottle she was lifting to her lips. She took a good swig and put it down. The bottle was almost empty.

I wanted to go home. I wanted to get away from the city, the apartment, the smoke that was filling it. Get away from drunken women who made passes at boys half their age. Mostly, right then, I wanted to kill Roger.

"I'm kidding, of course. I'm already married." She thumbed toward the living room. "Married to that thing out there. Have you paid homage yet? You must pay homage if you are to eat his food."

She was a pretty woman. Short and a little bit round, with wild dark hair. She had diamond-and-ruby earrings and several gold chains around her neck. Money, no power. Maybe that's what caused the bitterness.

"Are you Wendell's wife?"

111

"I am Wendell's wife, and that is Wendell's child." She nodded toward the baby in the doorway. The baby's chubby legs had ceased bouncing, and the seat twirled slightly. "I'm Wanda."

We shook hands, and I repeated my offer to help. Chopping onions would be more fun than listening to strangers argue.

As soon as I was busy with the knife, Wanda disappeared with her bottle. I finished with the pile she'd left me, then minced the garlic cloves. Dump it all in the sauce, she'd said. I knew better. I hunted in the cupboards for the right pan to use for sautéing. The baby followed me with his wide eyes.

Every few minutes someone came through the kitchen to go to the bathroom down the hall. No one offered to help, though they all offered me tokes off their joints. I hoped no one needed a revolution tonight; the people who could make it happen would be in no shape to do anything.

"Now, Jeffrey," I chided myself as I scraped the perfectly sautéd onions and garlic into the simmering sauce, "you have not earned that cynicism."

I turned to repeat this observation to the baby. I froze when I saw him. The little guy was sitting stone still in the bouncer. He was pale, droopy-eyed, and had some white stuff dribbling out of his mouth. I crouched to take a good look. His head lolled to the side.

Wanda walked through the kitchen, another bottle in hand. I put a hand on her arm. "The baby doesn't look too good," I said.

She waved me away. "He can stay in there for hours. He just loves to bounce." She turned into the bathroom and slammed the door.

I looked into the living room where Wendell was holding forth. The discussion had intensified. I tried to signal Roger, but he and all the others were oblivious to anything but the words rolling off tongues.

I put my hands around the baby just under his arms. I had never held a baby before, and I wasn't all that sure how to do it. I lifted, and he came out of the bouncer. He didn't slip or anything, so I raised him up, looked into his eyes, and saw lifeless, dilated pupils. I saw Gumbo. "Damn," I whispered. "This kid is stoned."

The smoke had nearly sickened me, and my lungs were probably five times as big as this little guy's. We both needed fresh air.

I set him into the crook of my right arm. I'd seen people do that, and it felt right. There was a back door off the kitchen that led to a small porch and rickety stairway. I figured it had to be safer than smoke city.

We were four stories up, and there was a pretty view. There were treetops and rooftops, and occasionally a bright-colored leaf drifted by. Baby's feet bounced, and I looked at him. He stared right back, already clear-eyed. I hoisted him up a bit higher in my arm and pointed. "Over there," I said, "is the Mississippi River. The big guys have made a mess of it, Baby, but if you go a little bit north or a little bit south it's still pretty and even sort of wild in spots. Worth checking out when you're older."

He bounced his legs again and waved his arms, and at that moment I discovered something I'd never known. I liked babies. Okay, sure, this was the first one I'd ever known, but he was such a sweet specimen that I was willing to extend my good feelings to all of them. I liked babies. I liked the way this one looked at me straight on for a while before smiling. No false friendliness. I liked this solid weight in my arms. I liked the soft brush of hair against my cheek. I liked the punch of his fat little fist.

Inside the apartment, someone screamed, someone bellowed, glass shattered. The arguing crescendoed, and I heard Roger's voice rise: "No, no, we *can* find common ground!"

Baby spoke: "Eeyup, goo, seee." Then he laughed.

I laughed, too. "Damn right, kid. They may be visionaries, but they are kind of silly." I nuzzled his nearly bald head. "And you deserve so much better."

• Part III •

Peace Comes Dropping Slow

· 1 ·

Maud Dougherty met Jeff Ramsey in the parking lot of the National Guard Armory in Red Cedar, Minnesota, on the second day of May 1970. She had driven two hours to the small town with a friend, Natalie Rinaldi. Natalie was dating the bass player in a band called Napalm that was playing at the armory. She had pleaded with Maud to drive, explaining that riding with the band was unpleasant and dangerous.

Maud didn't doubt that. She'd seen the band's van, an old, rusted VW bus with diseased exhaust. And she knew that the driver, the group's drummer who'd taken the stage name of Sticks, was a heavy drug user.

Still, she might have told Natalie to take her chances if it weren't for the fact that for several months they had been best friends. Natalie was the reason Maud did anything and went anywhere.

Last fall, when it seemed that the counseling Maud had finally agreed to was not accomplishing anything, Natalie, two years older and a student of Maud's father, had asked Maud to assist with a drama class for preschoolers at a community center.

117

Faced with another session with her counselor ("Let's hold hands, Maud; release your anguish through me"), Maud agreed.

At that first class, Natalie had spent most of the time on the phone with the bass player. Maud sat in a circle with the preschoolers. They waited, staring.

"Let's hold hands," she finally said. They obeyed.

"Let's release our . . ." Anguish?

A girl tittered. "Let's release our giggles," Maud said, "by bouncing on our butts."

She soon discovered the drawback of creating hysteria among four-year-olds: everyone needed a nose wipe. After cleaning up the faces, she taught them how to imitate vegetables.

By early December, Maud was at the center every day, often skipping school and always ignoring homework as she committed more and more time to volunteering. She argued with her father about dropping out of school.

Don't be stupid, he had said.

School is stupid, answered Maud. She wouldn't go, he couldn't make her.

Finally, he had negotiated with the high school administration to give her credit for her work at the center. In January, Maud was put on the payroll when the center started receiving special federal money for inner-city programs. "They're just giving it away!" the center's director, George, said at a staff meeting. "And what *we* get, they can't spend on the war!" Maud earned minimum wage, $1.60 an hour, and her days were full.

So when Natalie asked her the favor, Maud agreed. She owed something.

The Red Cedar armory was a new brick building at the edge of town. Maud had spent most of the night sitting on the entryway floor. She hated Napalm's music. No harmony, no melody, no unity of music and lyrics — just interminable drum and bass solos. She was more familiar with the group's music than she cared to be because she had often gone with Natalie to hear Napalm play in clubs around the Twin Cities. She had guessed she'd be bored tonight and she'd brought a book, *Anna Karenina*. It was slow reading, however, because Maud wasn't too sympathetic to Anna and she kept losing interest. Destruction by passion just didn't make sense. For the tenth time in two hours, she put the book aside. Thinking about the ill-fated heroine, she closed her eyes and dropped her head on her arms. What sort of vegetable did Anna resemble? Something crisp and flavorful, but easily rotted.

"Dammit, kid, I've told you for the last time to get those flyers out of here. And *you* get out of here. You're not comin' back."

Maud looked up just as a uniformed security guard lifted his stick and jabbed at the chest of a tall boy. "Out," the guard shouted. "Get the hell out!"

Maud frowned. While sitting in the entry she'd seen plenty of suspicious-looking people. But this guy could only be described as clean-cut. His clothes were ironed and he had short hair. Maud didn't know when she'd seen ears on a boy her own age.

119

The guard shoved the boy. Watching, Maud tensed. The boy took a breath and calmly stood his ground. The guard then grabbed the stack of papers the boy was holding. "These stay here. I have the perfect place for them."

Concern washed over the boy's face, then gathered into a slight, worried smile. "Please let me have them. I'll leave, but let me have the flyers. The mimeo broke and I can't make another batch."

"Isn't that too bad?" The guard tossed them into a trash can. "I know who you are, kid. You oughta be ashamed of what you're doing. Your brother died and you do this. Now get out. I don't want any disruptions, hear me?"

Maud rose and walked to the trash can.

The boy raised his hand. "I paid. I've been stamped. I can go in."

"Get out."

Several people had gathered to watch the confrontation. The boy turned to them and smiled. "We'll be protesting the invasion of Cambodia tomorrow at the parade. Meet at the courthouse at two and bring —"

The guard shoved hard, and the boy stumbled toward the door. The bystanders headed back into the music. Doors opened, and the sound of pounding drums rolled out.

Maud lifted a flyer out of the trash. The words were carefully hand-lettered.

Dissent Is Loyal
Protest the Invasion
of Cambodia
Tomorrow at the
VFW Loyalty Day Parade
Meet at the Courthouse
2:00 P.M.
Sunday May 3

Maud picked up the stack of flyers and slipped them inside her jacket. She zipped, retrieved her book, then hurried past the guard who stood watching at the door.

She looked about in the dark before spotting a tall figure walking away through the cars. Running after him, she held one arm against her chest to keep the flyers from slipping through. "Wait," she called. "I've got them. I've got your papers."

He halted and turned. She pulled the flyers out of her jacket. "I thought you'd like them. If you want, I could go back in and hand them out, but even if the guard didn't catch me doing it, I think people would just trash them; they're here for music."

He nodded. "I suppose you're right."

"We could put them on the cars," Maud said. "Under the wipers."

He looked behind her at the building. "That guard might still be watching."

She placed the flyers in his hand. "I'll go talk and distract him. Work fast."

The guard was happy to tell Maud about restaurants. Onion rings, malts, seafood — evidently the small town had the best of everything.

Want sweet rolls? Be sure to try . . .

Hungry for pie? There's only one place . . .

Malts and fries? Everyone goes . . .

He was writing down directions for a place called the Riviera when Maud looked out and saw a shadow jumping and waving its arms.

"Thanks so much," she said. The guard handed her the directions with a wink, then started discussing steak houses with the ticket-taker.

The jumping shadow had disappeared, and Maud walked slowly among the cars. She was just about to kick a tire and go back inside when he slid off the hood of a car and stood up. "Thanks," he said. "I distributed them all. Could have used more."

Maud looked around and didn't see any papers on windshields.

"I put them inside the cars," he said. "For safety. After these concerts, people are so stoned or dopey from the music that they might drive away without noticing the paper on the windshield."

Maud nodded. She knew what he meant, exactly. She checked her watch. Ten-thirty. Napalm was scheduled to play for another hour, then there'd be some take-down time. She could be pretty sober for the drive home if she smoked now. This guy looked a little straight, but these days it really was impossible to tell. Maud fished in her pocket, felt the joint, rolled it in her fingers.

"Did you break into the cars?" she asked.

"It's a small town. No one locks."

"I did. But I'm from Minneapolis."

He frowned. "You drove a hundred miles to hear this band?"

"My friend is the bass player's girlfriend. I'm her chauffeur."

He offered his hand. "Jeff Ramsey."

She quickly pulled hers out of the pocket, and the joint went flying onto the ground. Jeff looked at it. "You're lucky that didn't happen when you were talking to the guard."

Maud picked it up. It was coated with oily grit. She ripped it in two and let the brown flakes scatter. She wiped her hand and shook his. "Maud Dougherty. Would you like to go someplace for coffee or something? I hate this band, and I have to wait for my friend." She held up the fat book in her hand. "And I've had enough of Russian melancholy."

He took the novel and held it close to his face to read the title in the dark. "Huh. I've never read Tolstoy or any other Russians. I like German writers, though. I read them."

"Hesse, I bet."

"*Steppenwolf* is my favorite. I've read it three times."

"I liked *Siddhartha* better."

Jeff shook his head vigorously and widened his stance, preparing for a literary bout. "But *Steppenwolf* is far more effective, I think . . ."

Cars speeding past on the nearby highway threw

swipes of shadow and light across them. While Jeff critiqued what he called the novelist's methodology in presenting philosophical issues, Maud studied his face. "Why don't we talk somewhere else?" she said when he paused to catch his breath.

"I'm sorry." He dropped his head, then looked up at her and smiled. "I get carried away."

"Is there a restaurant nearby? The guard mentioned one called the Riviera."

"It's sort of a date den," he said. "Small booths and low lights. There's a place not far from here. But I didn't drive."

"I did. Let's go."

Jeff had difficulty getting into the front seat of Maud's car. She leaned to help him adjust the seat and they cracked heads, then when the seat shot back on its track his hand swiped her on the face.

"Gosh, I'm sorry. This is the first time I've ridden in a Japanese car. Does it break down a lot?"

"Never. And it uses about zero gas."

His knees pressed against the dash. "Maybe we should walk."

Maud backed up, shifted, let the car leap forward. "Why walk when you can drive?"

Jeff smiled. "The American way."

He directed her to a truck stop, chatting all the time in a rather cheerful manner about the illegality of the latest war development. That afternoon President Nixon had revealed he'd ordered American troops into Cambodia for the purpose of destroying Communist strongholds. The evening papers, the radio announcers, and now this boy were consumed by the invasion.

Maud was concerned with other things. She looked at the rows of semis parked behind the restaurant. "Jeff, I'm not sure about this. I'm kind of suspicious about these places. My friend and I were following the band down this evening and we stopped at a truck stop because the band's van needed oil. We really got hassled. Truckers can be jerks."

"That's because you were with the band. Now you're with me. I've discovered that there are advantages to dressing like a teenaged Republican. I usually don't get hassled."

"I hope you're right," Maud said as she got out of the car. "I've already been called a hippie slut once today, and that's once too often."

"Really? Someone said that?"

"Someone in a truck stop."

Arms akimbo, he sighed and shook his head. "Maud, sometimes I just don't understand people. Do you ever have trouble with that?"

She was still laughing when she slid into a booth. He followed several steps behind.

"What was so funny?" he asked once he was seated across from her.

She thought about one possible response: his endearing naiveté. "Let's just say," she answered finally, "that I'm glad I met you tonight."

"Ditto."

She leaned forward on her arms and watched while he studied the menu. She bet he'd get pie. Apple pie.

She looked around and noted gratefully that no burly truckers were scowling at her or her companion. Not this time, not with this boy. He bumped his glass, water spilled, and he apologized with the same worried, or weary, smile she'd seen earlier. Maud knew at that moment that she wanted to remember all of this: the bright truck stop in the strange town, the adventure of outsmarting the guard, the sight of the long legs in the small car, this serious boy, her new friend.

The waitress arrived and said something, Jeff laughed, they ordered. Yes, apple pie.

Several times their conversation was interrupted by people who stopped by the booth and greeted Jeff.

"You are famous," Maud said. "Everyone seems to know Jeff Ramsey."

"It's a small town. All those people are friends of my mother's or brother's."

"Tell me about your brother. That guard said he'd died."

"Vietnam. Last summer."

Dead siblings. They had that in common. But his had died in uniform, a defender. How could she possibly tell him about her sister, who had died in an explosion of anger and dynamite?

Always safer, she believed, to ask rather than tell.

"Your brother dies in the war and you organize a protest. Isn't that a little unusual?"

"Too much so." He pushed away his empty pie plate and tapped on the table with his index finger. "Protest has nothing to do with the soldiers. People

126

need to understand that. Today the president of my country expanded an illegal war by invading Cambodia. And you can be sure that when thousands of people cry out against it — and they will, Maud, they will — Nixon will as good as spit on us. We have a right to be heard and —"

"Hush, Jeff, you're shouting."

"Dissent is patriotic, Maud. Maybe it won't change things. Probably he'll stop the war only when it suits him; I know that. But those of us who think the war is immoral cannot be silenced by his scorn. Dissent is essential."

"Peaceful dissent."

He sat back and furrowed his brow. "Well, of course."

What followed was more talk that came more easily than any she'd ever had with anyone. They discussed their volunteer work, Maud's canoeing, his memories of first visiting a farm. Jeff was cheerfully describing his first encounter with a horse when Maud drifted into her own thoughts.

She reviewed her options: never see him again, spend a small fortune on phone bills and gas, move to Red Cedar. Unless, of course . . .

"Do you have a girlfriend?" she blurted. Might as well know.

"No, I don't," he said.

Thank God, she thought. "Oh," she said.

They were careful not to touch each other when they walked to the car, and they didn't speak until she drove into the nearly empty armory parking lot. Maud spotted Natalie standing by the van, which was one of the few vehicles remaining.

"It's later than I realized."

"Yes," he said softly.

"I should have taken you home."

"It's only four blocks, and it's a nice night for a walk."

Again they were careful not to touch as they walked from Maud's car to where Natalie stood with the band. The musicians were loading equipment, and Sticks was inspecting the engine.

"It's dead," Natalie said as a greeting.

"I can fix it," Sticks said. "But I need a part."

"There's a truck stop nearby," said Maud.

"Is that where you were?" said Natalie. She raised her eyebrows.

"They won't have import parts there," said Jeff. "The only place in town that carries anything like that is a small station that's closed. It might be open to-morrow."

"Damn," Sticks said, and he lit a cigarette.

"You're welcome to stay at my place." Jeff looked at Maud. "All of you."

"Far out," said Sticks. The others agreed.

"I'm not sure," said Maud.

"Oh, please," said Natalie, and she locked her hand onto Maud's arm. "I don't want to leave Bryan," she whispered, "but I don't want to stay alone with the guys."

Maud sighed. Sure, she owed her sanity to Natalie,

but to spend a night in a strange town with Napalm? She looked at Jeff. On the other hand . . .

"Won't your parents mind?" she asked.

"They're away this weekend. Fishing with friends on the Mississippi."

Natalie's grip tightened. "Okay," said Maud. "But I'll have to call my dad, and I'll probably wake him up."

Natalie squealed as the bassist gathered her in a hug. "Far out," he whispered as he kissed her several times on the ear.

Maud looked at Jeff and saw that he was happy.

· 2 ·

Jeff apologized for the mess as he let Maud and the others into his house. "I've been preparing for tomorrow," he explained. He smiled at Maud. "Making posters, the ultimate weapon."

Sticks picked up one of the pieces of cardboard and read, "It is loyal to dissent. U.S. Constitution guarantees free speech." He furrowed his brow and shook his mangy head of hair. "Little wordy for a slogan, isn't it?"

Jeff reached for the sign and ripped it in two. "You're right," he said grimly. "It's pretty lame."

"Don't get me wrong. I mean, the war's a real bummer and all. You gotta say it, right?" He tipped his head. "Ricardo here just got his notice. Best lead man in seven states, and he's gotta go tote a gun. What a waste. I'm 4-F, myself. Eyes, okay, not the queer thing." He reached into his pocket and pulled out a joint. "Can we smoke?"

Before Jeff could speak there was a loud knock on the door. Maud's stomach spinned. Cops. Undoubtedly, they'd been followed from the armory because someone had called in the suspicion that the band from Minneapolis was loaded with drugs and was staying to party in town. She knew that the band carried enough stuff to subdue the population of a college dorm. Napalm rehearsed stoned, performed stoned, traveled stoned.

And now, because she was loyal to Natalie and because she wanted to spend a little more time with a tall boy who had a worried smile, she was going to be busted in Red Cedar, Minnesota.

Please explain that, Maud.

But Dad, it's not as if I was caught with a bomb.

The door opened, and a boy poked his head in. "Jeff," he said, "are you having a party?"

Aside from Sticks's nauseating leg rubs in restaurant booths when she and Natalie went out with the band, Maud had not had any physical contact with a boy since she'd been with Ed. Nor had she desired any. But when she saw Jeff react to his new visitor by falling back into the sofa, his shoulders and smile collapsing in resignation, she longed to touch him. To reach out, trace the square line of his jaw with her thumb, press her palm against his chest. She yearned to sit back in his arms by a lakeshore and count stars in a dark summer sky. Inside, something was cooking.

"Hi, Gumbo," said Jeff. "Come on in."

The boy walked in, surveyed the room, looked puzzled, sat on the sofa by Jeff. "A party? With girls and everything?"

Jeff rolled his eyes. "Someone tell him."

Sticks did, finishing the tale by brandishing his joint. "And, like, I was just wondering if we could light up when you busted in."

Jeff rose. "And I was just about to say no. No drugs, and the girls sleep by themselves in one of the bedrooms." He squirmed, obviously uncomfortable with his rule-making. "It's my mother's house, and she . . ." He shrugged.

The bass player growled, and Natalie stiffened and frowned. Not what she'd planned on. Maud, however, relaxed entirely.

Gumbo nodded. "My friend is a priest, sort of, you know. That's why when I saw all the people coming in I had to check." He banged on Sticks's back. "I live right across the street, and my folks are gone fishing with Jeff's. Come on over. I've got some great Colombian, and if you don't have to get anywhere soon, you might want to drop a tab of Orange Marmalade. Great stuff, smooth trips."

The band left immediately. Natalie wavered, but when the bass player returned and tapped insistently on the front window, she smiled apologetically at Maud and then bolted.

"You're free to go," said Jeff. "I guess Gumbo is right. I am sort of a priest, only not really. Puritan, he used to call me. That's closer, I guess."

"Gumbo is a weird name."

"Yes, it is, but so is Pierre. He prefers Gumbo. Don't ask where it came from. No one remembers."

"He's an old friend?"

"My oldest. Practically a brother. I meant it about joining them, Maud. Feel free; my feelings won't be hurt."

"I'll stay, if it's okay. The guys aren't my favorite people. It's nicer here." And safer, she could have said.

"You said you needed to call your dad."

"I do. It's sort of old-fashioned, but it's one of the rules. And if I don't break them, anything else is okay."

He showed her the phone in the kitchen, then excused himself. Just as she feared would happen, she woke her father.

"Glad you called," he said. "I'll see you tomorrow."

She hung up the phone, sighed, and leaned against the wall. She enjoyed the freedom her father allowed her, but it was puzzling. Not all that long ago, there had been long lists of rules, curfews, and interrogations. Now she could travel with a rock band to a distant town and he didn't seem to care. She wondered if when her father lost Lucy, he'd let go of her as well.

She heard the squeak of marker on cardboard and joined Jeff in the other room. He glanced at her, took in her mood, and smiled sympathetically. "Family junk?" he asked.

She nodded, picked up a purple marker, and rolled it between her fingers. "May I help with the posters?"

"Would you? I don't want to force you into participating just because you're crashing here for the night."

Payback for a debt. Maud wet her lips and licked away a smile. What a strange boy. Any other guy she'd known — the band boys, hairy Ed, even dear old Keller — might have suggested a slightly more serious repayment.

She was embellishing the border of her third poster — HONOR OUR SOLDIERS BY BRINGING THEM HOME — when she heard Jeff swear softly and sigh deeply. "Damn," he said again.

She looked up. He had finished his posters and was now sitting with a long piece of black cloth across his lap. He snapped a ribbon of white elastic as he chewed on his lip.

"What's wrong?" she asked.

"I want to give out black armbands tomorrow, but I can't figure out a way to attach the elastic. Mom doesn't have a sewing machine, and I don't want to hand-stitch the things. Chrissake, it's nearly three." He closed his eyes and leaned back against the wall. "I don't know why I started all this."

Maud went to him. She picked up the cloth and ripped off a narrow band. "They don't have to be elaborate, Jeff. Just give people a strip of cloth, and they can tie them on. It'll work fine."

Jeff grabbed the cloth back and fiercely ripped strips that fell into a pile on his lap. When he finished he looked at her, glaring. Maud drew back, looked closely at him, and realized that the intensity of his glare was directed within.

"Sometimes," he muttered, "I complicate things that are really very simple. This is twice since I met you that you have had a better idea. First with the flyers, now the armbands. You're very practical, aren't you?"

Not always, Jeff. Flyers and armbands are easy, but sisters and bearded men and tall worried boys are a puzzle.

"I'm a good cook," she replied.

"That's not an answer. Man, it's late. Would you like to go to bed?"

In a melting warm rush Maud realized she did, but not in the way he certainly meant. "I guess so," she replied.

"I'll show you the room."

"The sofa is fine."

"And have that drummer come back when he's two hours into an acid trip and start singing into your navel? You can have the bedroom."

"You could lock the door."

"*You* can lock the *bedroom* door."

He gave her a T-shirt and even found a new tooth-brush. It was pink, with a flamingo carved out of the handle. "It's from my mother's honeymoon in Vegas."

"Won't she want to keep it?"

"She brought back a dozen."

In the brief time she was alone before turning out the lights, she explored his room. It was clean and orderly and spare in its decorations. There was a huge peace-sign poster, pictures on the bureau, piles of books, twin beds. Nothing needed dusting.

She lay in the dark on the bed across from the peace

sign. The other bed was obviously his. Unmade, it was the only messy spot in the room.

She wondered why she hadn't told him about Lucy, who wasn't exactly a minor detail. After only four hours together they had certainly talked about everything else. She'd told him about her mother, why not her sister? It would have been so simple: Do you remember last summer . . .

He would remember, of course. Just as the guard knew about Jeff's brother, Jeff would know about Lucy. Everyone did.

She hadn't told him, she knew, because she hadn't wanted him to be like the others, all those others who so quickly chimed in with an opinion. A hero, a fool, wicked or brave.

No, she didn't want him to be like all the others.

Maud rolled onto her side and looked at the poster. The colors had disappeared into the dark, but the circle and lines were visible. Footprint of the American chicken was how hardhats loved to describe it. The peace sign was probably the last thing he saw each night.

She wasn't at all sleepy. She wanted to talk. She was going to tell him, she decided. She was going to go straight up and say, My sister blew up a building and died while protesting the war your brother fought and died in.

Whadda ya think, Jeff? Do you want to tell me what it all means? Do you understand it? Do you have any idea what Lucy was thinking as she sat and waited, tick, tick, tick, for her life to end?

She didn't know if it would be a challenge or a confession. Either way, she wanted him to know.

He was asleep on the sofa. All the lights were on. She stood over him, looking and memorizing. White T-shirt and olive green boxers. His chest rose slightly with each breath. His fingertips were marker-stained. There was a purple streak under his chin.

Maud turned out the lights. She looked out the front window and saw that in the house across the street the lights were burning and people were dancing. Fifty yards, no farther than that, but to Maud's way of measuring, it was a world miles away.

· 3 ·

It was warm and sunny the next afternoon when Maud and Jeff met the other war protesters on the courthouse lawn in Red Cedar. While Jeff solicited people to hold posters, Maud distributed armbands. Soon there was a cluster of black-banded people amidst the larger crowd of parade-goers. After all of the demonstrators had been handed cloth strips, Maud turned to the other people waiting on the street.

"Loyalty shouldn't be blind," she said as she offered an armband to a gray-haired lady who was walking through the protesters. The woman shook her head, pursed her lips, and regripped her handbag as she hurried past Maud.

Maud acknowledged that the woman might feel uncomfortable; the group of demonstrators did look unsavory. There was plenty of long hair, ripped jeans, beards, and beads. Gumbo and the band members had set up lawn chairs on the sidewalk where the courthouse lawn met Main Street. They were reclining and drinking lemonade.

Maud held out an armband to a long-haired boy who grabbed it, dropped it, and spat. "Nice day for a parade," Maud said. The boy muttered an obscenity and spat again before walking on.

Maud counted heads. Twenty-five, maybe thirty people in their group. That was it. A whole night of leafleting and poster making, and not even three dozen protesters had shown up. There were plenty of others, though. Main Street was crowded with parade watchers.

Jeff didn't look discouraged. "Perfect weather," he said as he approached Maud. "Could I have some of those armbands? I want to run them down to the staging area. I know some kids in the school band who might want them."

She handed over half her supply. "Do you suppose many more people will join us?"

"I'm surprised this many showed up. It's a pretty conservative town. Oh, man, look at that, Maud!"

Nearly a dozen men carrying American flags were assembling directly across the street.

Jeff waved and shouted. "Hi, Mr. Taylor. Hi, Mr. Wassel. Nice day for a parade."

Maud socked him on the arm. "Stop it. You're only going to provoke them."

He nodded. "They hate it when you're nice. But I know most of those guys, Maud. They work at the plant with my mom and her husband. Family friends."

"They don't look very friendly."

"No, they don't. And I bet they'll really go nuts when they see that we have a flag, too. Gumbo brought his parents' old one. Forty-eight stars. Oops — five minutes to showtime. I've got to hurry. Be back."

She didn't want him to go, not for even a few minutes. Faced with the scowling flag holders, surrounded by strangers in a strange town, Maud regretted for the zillionth time that she had agreed to stay for the parade. Not that there had been too much choice. After sleeping late, she had spent the morning shuttling a dopey Sticks between a service station and his van. It was after noon when the van finally returned to life.

"Might as well stay for the parade, help out Jeff," said Sticks. "How 'bout you girls? Wanna stay?"

"Oh yes!" said Natalie. She turned to Maud. "Please?"

"We'll make it a party," said Gumbo, and the band murmured approval.

"Please, please!" said Natalie. "The van could break down," she whispered in Maud's ear. "If we're not there to help, some rednecks might stop and give the guys a bad time."

"Do what you want," said Jeff, and he kneeled down to stack posters and collect markers. That left Maud cold, until he rose and she saw, she believed, a different message in his eyes.

"Okay," she said, "but I'll have to call home again."

Gumbo, Natalie, and the band *had* made a party of it and were now reveling on the lawn chairs. Jeff had disappeared, and Maud was left holding armbands.

A police car crawled down the street toward them, and stopped directly in front of the lawn chairs. The cop slid an elbow out the open car window, scowled, and tugged on the brim of his hat. "No trouble!" he growled. "I don't want any trouble."

A protester shouted back at him, and there were concurring murmurs. The flag wavers across the street started calling names.

Gumbo jumped out of his chair and stepped in front of the protester who had shouted at the cop. "Cut the crap, man," he said. "You're not gonna ruin things by blowing off your mouth." Gumbo picked up a poster from the stack of extras. "Hold this and keep quiet."

The man took the poster and held it high overhead. Across the street the shouting intensified.

Gumbo sat back down. "Hey, Sticks," he said, "hand me that tanning lotion."

Jeff returned, breathless and red from running. "The music director took all the armbands and trashed them! He said anyone who wore one while marching would be kicked off the band. What a waste."

There was a sudden burst of band music, which brought everyone but the lawn-chair party to attention. "The flag," said Jeff. "Let's get the flag out." He pulled a box from under the chairs, opened it, and lifted out a faded flag wrapped around a short pole. He stood on the curb and waved it. Maud stood next to him, and all around them black-banded protesters held posters aloft and cheered. "Let's be the loudest," Jeff said.

The parade was composed mostly of units of war veterans from small towns in the area, interspersed with school bands. An elaborate float depicting last summer's moon landing received loud cheers and applause. Maud noticed that whenever a contingent of vets passed the demonstrators, the marchers stiffened and scowled. No politician waved to her group; no clown threw candy.

The smallest unit of soldiers was a group of World War I veterans. They marched slowly in step. As they passed Jeff and the flag, one man in the front line turned his head, winked, and saluted.

The last band was an untuneful ensemble from a town Maud had never heard of. Behind that group of struggling musicians was a patrol car, followed by hundreds of satisfied and happy people who had spilled onto the street.

Jeff put an arm around Maud and hugged. "It was better than I hoped for. Did you see that one old guy who saluted?"

She was glad, at that moment, that she had stayed. Glad she could help him make his message a little louder, happy now to be standing on Main Street with day-old clothing and color-stained hands.

She returned his hug. "I didn't tell you this before, but it was my very first demonstration."

"Yes," piped in Natalie, who had appeared at her side. "Now you're not a virgin."

Maud turned, ready to slug her friend senseless, but before she could even catch her breath, out of the corner of her eye she saw Jeff go stumbling backward.

"What the hell?" Jeff shouted.

The flag wavers had come across the street. One of

them had a grip on Jeff's flag. "This doesn't belong with scum," he said.

Jeff held fast.

"Your brother died for this flag," the man said, yanking.

Jeff pulled hard.

The man lifted a leg and kicked Jeff just as he yanked again.

The pole cracked and split, Jeff stumbled and fell, and his head hit hard on the sidewalk. The man tumbled, and the jagged edge of the broken pole was driven across Jeff's face and down his chest.

The crowd closed in, and Maud lost her view of the scene. She pushed forward and was shoved back by a man with a flag. She crouched to look through legs and saw Jeff, motionless and bloody.

She rose and pushed and was shoved back again. There were taunts and jeers and screams.

"Police!"

"An ambulance!"

She heard Gumbo shriek: "You son of a bitch!" And just as Maud finally found her way through to the opening around the body, she saw Gumbo lift up, then attack the man who had struggled with Jeff. She saw him hit with his fists again and again and again. The man dropped to his knees, and the flag fell into the gutter. Gumbo spun around. He knelt and gathered Jeff in his arms and rocked.

Maud stood with the crowd — now silent and immobile — and watched as the tears of one boy mixed with the blood of another.

An ambulance took Jeff, and a cop took Gumbo. The other man was hustled away by a protective circle of friends. One police officer stayed behind, taking names and making notes of the different versions of the incident.

Along with the others who lingered, Maud gave her name and address. "I saw it all," she said.

The officer was unimpressed. "You head back to Minneapolis," he said. "All of you, just get out of town."

Maud wanted to stay and go to the hospital, but the others protested.

"I've got two lids of dope in the van," said Sticks. "There's bound to be cops at the hospital, and I don't want to be stopped and searched. You saw how that pig looked at us. He said go, and I wanna go."

"I'll stay."

"Maud!" pleaded Natalie.

She gave in, acknowledging to herself that there was nothing she could do. Nothing she could change or fix by staying one moment longer in the sorry little town.

The van cruised at seventy all the way to Minneapolis. Maud dropped Natalie off at the bass player's apartment. She honked twice at the boys as they began to unload equipment, then drove away.

"This was the last time," she said loudly, "that I go anywhere with a band. My life as a groupie is over." She reached for the radio dial, turned it on, and searched through the stations until she found the peaceful sounds of a baseball game.

Her house was empty. There were rolls on the counter and a note on the refrigerator: "Dinner with my honors students. Home by ten."

She showered. In slightly more than twenty-four hours she had acquired a stew of odors, mostly from cigarettes and sweat. Standing rigid under the steaming stream, she held her breath and closed her eyes, hoping all the smells and images would be washed away.

She tightened the lock on her eyelids and lifted her face into the water. Brain pictures were still vivid and she saw it all — the flags, the blood, Jeff lying in his friend's arms.

What if he were dead? He could be; his head had hit hard.

"No!" she cried out, and water ran into her mouth and down her throat. She bent over, coughing and crying while water streamed over her.

Maud made herself wait until after nine before calling. The operator had to twice repeat the number before Maud got it right. Then she dialed. Five times. She'd let it ring five times, that's all.

A woman answered on the first ring, and Maud hung up.

Stupid, she thought. Then she dialed again.

"Well, what?" a woman snapped into the phone.

"Hello," said Maud. "I'm a friend of Jeff's from

145

Minneapolis, and I wanted to see how he was doing. Is he okay?"

She heard a deep inhalation, a murmur, a man's voice in the background. Then:

"Honey, sorry about the mean hello. But I've been getting the nastiest calls since I walked in the door."

"Are you his mom?"

"That's right. Jeff's okay. Twenty-three stitches altogether, chest and face, and he banged up his brain. They let him come home, and he's sleeping it off. Tomorrow he won't feel any worse than I do the morning after a good toot. What's your name, hon?"

"Maud. What about Gumbo?"

"He's home, too. The police couldn't figure out what to charge him with. I tell you, that's the last time we grown-ups go fishing. I'll tell Jeff you called. I don't know you, do I?"

"No."

"Maybe someday. Thanks for calling, hon."

Maud turned off the lights and went to her room. She sat on her bed and looked out the window. Their house was on a hill, and she could see the lights of the city and the river of headlights from the nearby highway.

As she so often did, she thought of Lucy and her sister's years of rebellion and running. She imagined — again — the horrifying image of her sister's death, then recalled the loud, proud demonstrators at that afternoon's parade. She could still hear the jeering, angry hecklers with their wounded patriotism. Closing her eyes, she saw Jeff, still and bloody, surrounded by the shocked and silent people of his hometown.

Her father entered the house, and Maud rose to go back downstairs. She was exhausted, but knew he'd want to see her to exchange news and say good night.

And how was your day, Maud?

Gosh, Dad, let me tell you . . .

And she *would* tell him — all about the flyers and the guard and the armbands, about the posters, the flag, the beating. She'd tell it all, tell him the latest developments in the never-ending story of the long, sad war.

· 4 ·

The little girl was crying. Maud set down the basket she'd been carrying to the community center's storeroom and stroked the girl's face.

"What's wrong, Gaby?"

"Crawford. He . . . he . . ." She collapsed into Maud's arms.

Maud comforted the child with murmurs and a long hug as she looked over the head of red curls. Crawford was sitting at the table, quietly folding his napkin into a little square. Maud wasn't fooled by his innocent concentration. If anyone in the group was likely to cause a disruption it was Crawford.

"What did he do?" Maud asked.

Indignation overcame hysteria, and Gaby stamped her foot. "He lifted up my shirt," she said, "and put a peanut in my bellybutton."

One of the first things Maud had learned when she began working with the children at the center was how to stifle laughter. She did it now with three quick gulps of air.

"Well," she said slowly, "let's take a look."

"Not here!" Gaby said. They went to the bathroom.

148

The four-year-old locked the door carefully, closed her eyes, and lifted her shirt.

"The peanut is gone," said Maud.

Gaby looked down. She had a lovely, pale potbelly with a mole just above the navel. "Did it go inside, Maud?"

"I don't think so, sweetheart. It probably fell onto the floor."

Gaby dropped her shirt. "If I find it can I eat it?" She scowled. "It was my last peanut."

Maud unlocked the door and pushed it open. "No, you can't. But I'll get you some more from the kitchen." Gaby, cheered, skipped away. As she rounded the corner of the snack table to take her seat, she poked Crawford. He looked at her and burped.

As Maud walked down the hall to the kitchen, Natalie stepped out of the director's office. She waved her in with a snap of her wrist. "Inside. Fast," she hissed.

"What's up?"

Natalie just shook her head and pulled on Maud's arm. Inside the office, all of the staff was crowded around a desk where George, the director, sat. There was a radio on his desk, and he gripped it with both hands.

"We just heard," Natalie whispered tersely, "that in Ohio the National Guard started shooting at some demonstrators. They've killed people, Maud!"

"Hush!" George ordered.

"This just in," the radio announcer said in a tightly strung voice. "We have official confirmation of four deaths on the campus of Kent State University. This is official: four demonstrators protesting the invasion of Cambodia have been killed by the Ohio National Guard. It's not known —"

People swore and shouted. George threw a book against the wall. Maud leaned against the door frame. Just two days before, she'd watched Jeff get beaten up on the main street of his hometown. Now this.

"What's next?" Natalie said. "Will they be dropping bombs on peace rallies? Is Nixon bringing home the troops just to set them loose on campuses? What the hell is next?" The talking crescendoed into a cacophony of invective and threats. Just as Maud was about to turn away, she felt urgent tugging on her jeans. She looked down and saw Gaby.

"Everyone's done with snack, Maud. Can we do vegetables now? You promised we could do vegetables."

Maud dropped to her knees and hugged the little girl. "Yes, Gaby. We can do vegetables. We'll do them all — for as long as you want."

Maud watched as Gaby rushed back and shared the news with her classmates. They squealed and shouted, and Crawford turned cartwheels. Behind Maud, the radio voice rose above all others: Four dead. Four dead. Four dead.

"The demonstrators destroyed a campus building yesterday, and today they were throwing rocks!" Mr. Dougherty slammed his fist down on the table, spilling coffee, soup, and wine.

"That's no excuse for gunning them down," said Maud.

"Should we tolerate violence from the protesters just because we agree with their position on the war?" He sat back and glowered at Maud. "Is that what you think?"

Maud didn't know what to think, at least about this scene in the kitchen. Since she got home they'd been locked into a ceaseless argument. Guns! Rocks! Guns! Rocks! Pointed fingers and loud voices. She hadn't eaten much.

She calmed herself by breathing deeply, then she mustered a smile. A false one, but the best she could do. "I cooked; you clean."

He, too, was ready for a cease-fire. "Of course. Oh, Lord," he groaned and raised his hand. "I forgot. You got a call, and I took the message." He pointed at the refrigerator. "There it is."

"Thanks for telling me."

"You sound exactly like Lucy when you get sarcastic. I would have told you about the call, but you stormed in here from work steaming and ready to fight."

"*I* was ready to fight?"

"You had killer eyes, Maudie." The comment and the touch of his hand on her cheek won a true smile from Maud. He turned, unclipped the note from a magnet, and handed it to her.

Maud looked at the two-word message: Jeff called. She kept looking long enough to have memorized a stanza of Persian poetry. She excused herself and went upstairs to her room. Her heart raced as she dialed his number. "Not his mother," she said. "Please, not his mother."

His mother answered. "Hello-ho!"

"Jeff, please."

"Sure, honey," the woman said. "Hey, sweetheart," she called, "it's for you. I think it's that girl from Minneapolis. You didn't tell me if she was cute."

Dead mothers, thought Maud, aren't always so awful.

She counted to fifteen before he picked up the phone.

"It's Maud," she said.

"Sorry to keep you waiting. I had to dismember my mother and stuff her into a bag. How are you?"

Four dead in Ohio, the world's worst war going on, and a nasty, unfinished argument in her own house, but at that moment the problem puzzling Maud was, How did such a deep voice come from such a thin boy?

"I'm fine. How are you? I nearly died, Jeff, when you got beat up. It was so awful."

"I'm okay. The stitches and bruises look pretty gross, and I might have a couple of scars."

"What about Gumbo?"

"Nothing's going to happen. I said I wouldn't press charges against the guy who got me if he didn't go after Gumbo. The guy's brother bowls with my step-father. They worked it out."

"Peace through bowling? That's kind of funny."

"Maybe they should try it at the negotiations in

Paris. Nothing else is working. Maud, have you heard today's news?"

"Of course. It just gets worse, doesn't it? What happened to you was so awful. And now this."

"I heard on the radio that there's a march in the Twin Cities planned for Saturday."

"I suppose. I hadn't heard."

"It's all futile, but what else is there?"

Bowling, she wanted to say.

"I want to drive up for the march and rally. Would you go? Could we go together?"

A date? Their first date?

"I really don't know my way around Minneapolis," he continued. "The last time I was there I came with a friend, but now he lives in Georgia. I know I'd get lost."

Okay, it wasn't exactly an invitation to prom, but no one went to proms anymore anyway. "I'd like that, Jeff."

"It could be fun."

"Don't bring a flag this time."

She gave him directions to her house. He made her repeat them twice, and it was so easy to picture him writing carefully, concentrating on the details of her directions.

"I'll be there," he said.

Maud knew she could count on that. She knew that he'd be prompt, neatly groomed, intent, and cheerful. He wouldn't fail her.

Everyone Maud knew or encountered that week was distressed and angry. The same cries echoed everywhere: Four dead! Killing our own! Ohio, Ohio, Ohio.

Maud's spirits, however, rose higher each day as she anticipated seeing Jeff again. She felt energized. At home she washed windows and prepared and froze two weeks' worth of meals. At the center, she devised new activities for the kids and volunteered to accompany the senior citizen group on a field trip to a noodle factory.

On Friday afternoon (only twenty more hours!), she left the center early and met with her counselor at school. She reviewed her work at the center with him, and he assured her she'd graduate with her class.

"College, Maud?" he asked. "Once you were thinking about going out east."

Who cares about college, she thought. I'm just thinking about tomorrow. "I kind of forgot to take my SATs," she said.

He nodded, remembering her state of mind in the fall and her failure at school. He'd recorded it all in preparation for a professional paper he'd be giving that summer at a conference, when he'd lead a workshop on Meeting the Needs of the Needy Student. Maud, who would never be named, was his star example.

"Dad and I agree that postponing school for a year won't hurt. I'm in no hurry. I plan to keep working at the center. There's really more to learn there than in freshman English."

He nodded. "Very wise. I'm so glad things are going better."

Were they? Four dead. Of course, she had a date for tomorrow. "So am I. Thanks for your help, Mr. Huttner."

She left on wings. She was out. Done. Free. High school was now a memory.

On Saturday, just as Maud expected, Jeff arrived on time. And he was dressed as she expected. Frat boy, she thought. The cutest darn thing she'd ever seen.

They shook hands, and she clucked over his wounds. He shifted his weight back and forth over his feet. "Maud," he said, "are you going to let me in?"

She blushed and opened the door wider. He stepped in and looked around. "Great house."

Maud chuckled. "Yes, it's a very attractive foyer. Those chipped tiles are over seventy years old."

"I'm nervous, okay?"

"Me, too."

"I'm glad to see you. Even if this march hadn't been going on I might have driven up." He rubbed his palms together. "It's all sort of weird."

"Weird?"

"You . . ."

"I'm weird? Thank you, Jeff."

"I mean, what's weird is wanting to drive a hundred miles to see someone just because she had good ideas about leaflets and armbands."

Leaflets and armbands. How sexy. She made a mental list of the reasons why she'd drive to see him: his calm, his anger-free intensity, his deep voice.

155

And of course, she'd seen him in his boxer shorts.

"It's time to meet my father," she said.

She shouted twice for her father before she heard him descend from his study. "He hides on the third floor," she explained to Jeff, then wished she hadn't said it.

"Hides from what?"

Life. Change. Arguments. "Doing dishes," she answered. "Today is his day."

Mr. Dougherty shook Jeff's hand while being introduced, and he seemed unwilling to let go. "I'm a professional with words," he said, "but I can't begin to express how awful I feel about what happened to you at that parade. Maud told me all about it."

Jeff pulled his hand free and tucked it into his pocket. "Thank you, sir."

"Tired, stupid, old men like me," he said, "have let an immoral war get out of hand, and now it has a home front. And our children are the casualties."

"Will you come with us today?" asked Jeff.

"No. I'm not one for marching. A skeptic, I guess. But that doesn't mean I disapprove of those who do march. I don't judge the choices others make."

"Unless they choose to use rocks," said Maud. "Then he judges like hell."

"He's right," said Jeff. "If we don't speak up about that sort of violence . . ."

Maud sighed inwardly while he talked. These days everything generated examination and discussion. She couldn't even introduce someone resembling a boyfriend to her father for the first time in her life without it deteriorating into a political discussion. Enough. "I meant it as a joke. Let's just go."

"Sure," said Jeff. "It was nice to meet you, Mr. Dougherty."

"I hope you visit again."

"I'd like to. Seeing this neighborhood makes me wish I were going to the U. of M. next fall instead of St. Cloud State. The city might be interesting. There's so much going on, and it's so beautiful. The river, and all these great neighborhoods with old houses. Nothing like this in Red Cedar. This house and that painting. Nothing like *that* at home. I don't know anyone there who has a nude . . ." He stopped, suddenly embarrassed by the rush of words.

"Maud's mother did that painting. She was an artist."

"Is that her?" Jeff pointed to a photo in a silver frame.

"Yes."

Jeff stepped closer to the display of family pictures. "Maud, this is you, right? Man, you used to be cute. Who's this with you?"

"My sister, Lucy."

He rolled his head around and looked at her. Suddenly, she heard nothing but her heartbeat. Pum, pum, pum.

"I didn't know you had a sister. You didn't tell me that."

"We just met, sort of."

He nodded. "True. The two of you look a lot alike. Where does Lucy live?"

Maud and her father exchanged looks. She didn't doubt that inside he was feeling the same sinking.

"She's dead," said Mr. Dougherty. "She died last year."

Jeff paled and set down the picture. "Gosh, I'm so sorry."

Dead siblings, Jeff. Something in common.

"How?"

Maud and her father again looked at each other, then they both burst out laughing. Jeff looked utterly confused.

"I'm sorry, Jeff," said Mr. Dougherty. "It's just that we get so surprised when we find someone who doesn't know. That's why we laughed."

Maud slipped her arm through Jeff's. It didn't matter that she was in front of her father; she wanted to touch the boy. "My sister died when she blew up a building at the university. Suicide, I guess. A political one, if it makes a difference."

She felt Jeff stiffen. He turned and pulled away from her and looked again at the photograph. "I have no idea of what to say. I mean, yeah, I did know about it, but the name never registered, or maybe I just never paid attention. You see, right then . . ." He gave up. "I'm sorry," he whispered. "It's just awful. That's all."

"Don't feel you have to say anything," said Maud's father. "Sometimes, actually, it's better if people don't. But I'm sure you know that."

Jeff smiled, understanding. He sat on the edge of a chair. "Has it ever happened to either of you, since she died, that people just have to tell you what it all means? They can't stop with 'I'm sorry.' Like about my brother dying in the war. I get people who say he was a hero and other folks who call him a baby-killer. Everybody's got an opinion, and for some reason they're all compelled to tell me. No one comes close to the truth. My brother's dead. That's it. But people just can't resist telling me what they think. Do you ever get that from people?"

Mr. Dougherty started to speak, but faltered. Then he walked silently out of the room, pausing briefly to lay a hand on the boy's shoulder.

"I'm sorry," Jeff said to Maud. "I feel so stupid now. He had just told me I didn't have to say anything, and then I did, and of course I said something wrong."

She took his hand. "No," she said, pulling him up, "you said something right."

They drove to St. Paul to the college where Maud's father taught. It was the halfway point for the march, which began at the university and would end with a rally at the state capitol. The campus green was crowded with students and others who had decided to join the demonstration midway. People milled about, and a few played catch with tennis balls. Word went out: the marchers had been spotted a mile away, walking slowly uphill on the broad avenue that led from the Mississippi River.

Maud saw people she knew. She introduced Jeff to a few of them and shrugged off the inquiring looks of

159

girlfriends. Then she guided him through the crowd. "I have an idea," she said. "Follow me."

"You know this place pretty well."

"My dad has taught here since I was two." She opened up a dormitory door. "It's a second home."

He followed her up several flights of stairs and through a door. They stepped out onto the roof of the dorm.

"This is a favorite party spot," said Maud.

"Do you really party with college kids?"

"Sometimes. I get to know a lot of my father's students. They invite me." They leaned over the guardrail. Thousands of people were clustered below them. A few looked up and waved. People were chanting, waving posters, jogging in place. A balloon appeared and was passed overhead through the crowd. It hit a tree branch and popped.

Maud looked to her left and saw the front line of the march, a row of Vietnam veterans escorting a coffin that was painted with stars and stripes. The people on the campus grounds let a few hundred marchers pass, then, unwilling to wait any longer, surged onto the street. The chanting swelled into a roar that seemed to roll back all the way to the river.

"How many?" Maud asked Jeff.

"I have no idea. Ten thousand?"

"Sounds good."

"What the hell, let's make it twenty."

"Why not."

They didn't leave to join the march. It was as if, standing five stories high, they were attending a great

160

show. Detached and distant, they watched the players below.

They watched until the last marchers were out of sight, then kept watching as police removed wooden barriers from the cross streets. Signals flashed green, and traffic resumed its Saturday rush.

"What's the point, Jeff?" whispered Maud. "They could march all the way to Washington, a million of them, and it would do nothing. Why are we here?"

"The point," he said slowly, "is that if we don't do something, it will just get worse next time. If we don't speak out, it will be too easy for the politicians to believe they can get away with anything. And — maybe this is the most important reason — if we don't do something, take some action, we're only left with anger."

"Are you angry? You're the calmest person I've ever met."

"Of course I'm angry. Every day, I wake up and it's the same. It's like the whole world is filled with rage. I'm not immune. But if I don't do something — even something stupid like making posters — it just builds. You can go crazy with anger. Maybe that's really the bomb that killed your sister, Maud." He held out and cupped his hands, as if there were something in each. "Anger or action. If I just keep doing something, I feel like I have a choice. I feel like I have control."

Anger. Action. Maud grabbed his hand and pulled, and suddenly they were racing down the stairs. Outside, they ran down the sidewalk and across the street. Brakes squealed, horns honked.

The sounds of the march grew louder as they made up the distance. Just when Maud thought her lungs would burst and the rest of her body implode, she reached her goal. Jeff — longer legs, faster gait — was already there. He turned and smiled, held out a hand, and pulled her in.

· 5 ·

Maud fell asleep during the speeches at the rally. When the fifth politician approached the microphone to add his two cents' worth, she closed her eyes, leaned against Jeff, and dozed.

She was briefly roused whenever the incessant chants and shouts were unified into a roar. The first time it happened she blinked and wondered, What sort of dream is this? The second time, she sat erect, faced Jeff, and said, "Let's go camping. I want to sleep with you in a tent tonight." She was asleep again before he had even blushed.

She woke fully when Jeff gently tugged her braid. "I've heard enough," he said. "Ready to go?"

Maud unhooked her cramped legs from each other and tried to rise. She listed and wobbled, then grabbed Jeff's arm. She stamped her feet and shook her head.

"You okay?" said Jeff. "You're kind of acting like a horse."

Wide awake now. "You're the first person to ever compare me to a horse, Jeff. Sweet."

Someone stumbled against them before Jeff could respond. "Wow, man," the stranger said, "that was crude. I could've hurt you. Did I hurt you?" He spun around to Maud. "Did I hurt you? Good. Fine. Are we fine?"

Maud nodded.

"Smoke?" The stranger brandished a joint.

Maud frowned. He'd obviously had too much already. "Don't be stupid," she said and waved her hand toward the rally stage. "There are cops everywhere."

He whirled and offered the joint to Jeff. "Smoke one for peace." Jeff shook his head. The man shrugged and took a long hit. Jeff turned to Maud and raised his eyebrows. She nodded, and they slipped away.

"This is a great crowd," he said. "Even a better mix of people than last fall."

"I wasn't there," she said. "Remember, I told you the Red Cedar parade was my first protest."

"The armory was your first."

"Talking to a security guard?"

"Exactly. Taking action is the real protest. Not this." And he waved his arm to sweep across the scene.

A woman spun around. "I heard that. What do you think this is, then?"

"I think —"

"Of course it's real, and the forty thousand people here would agree with me." She turned to a companion. "This boy doesn't think this is a real demonstration." Her voice was harsh and loud, and people turned to listen. "He said . . ." she exclaimed.

"I meant . . ." Jeff answered.

164

Maud heard an angry undercurrent to the murmured comments coming from the people around them. Having just marched in confrontation to a distant, untouchable president, these people were like unsatisfied predators. Still seething, still hungry for blood, still angry. So they had turned on the one person among them who looked like a Republican.

"I suppose you think . . ."

"Please, what I was saying . . ." Jeff said.

Maud reached in. "Jeff," she said urgently, "I'm going to get sick." She clutched her stomach and swallowed hard. "Let's go." She moaned a bit, and the crowd split apart. Jeff took her hand, and they hurried away. When they reached the outer edge of the sea of protesters, they paused and he looked at her.

"Faking? Thought so. Well, you rescued me again."

"You weren't enjoying that argument, were you?"

"It wasn't even an argument. That would have been okay. It was . . . oh gosh, I don't know."

"A preliminary to a mauling."

He smiled. "Maybe. How far are we from the car?"

"I'd guess three miles."

He frowned. "Is there a bus?"

"I don't know."

"I thought you lived here."

"I live in Minneapolis. This is St. Paul. There's a big difference. I'm only familiar with the neighborhood Dad's college is in."

"I guess we walk."

Maud made a fist and wiggled the thumb. "Not

when we were born with these. Let's hitch. Out of all the people at this rally, someone must have planned ahead and left a car down here."

They crossed the street, stood on the corner, and stuck out thumbs. Even though the rally was far from being over, the crowd was dispersing. Several others were hitching and each time a car pulled over to offer a ride, ten hitchhikers rushed toward it.

"No way," Jeff said as he watched people pile into a Mustang. "I'm not going to sit on some strange guy's lap."

"Let's walk a bit."

"Do you know the way?"

"We can follow the march route." She pointed. "Let's walk as far as the cathedral. There won't be such a crowd there, and maybe drivers will think we're pious churchgoers and give us a lift."

They walked in silence. It had been a day of talk, and Maud savored the quiet. Still, she felt the urge to dig into Jeff's life. There were a million things she wanted to know. Pick carefully, Maud, she ordered herself. Should she ask about his mother? His father? Or his brother's death? Saddest memory? Scariest dream? How deep should she go?

"My feet are tired, Maud."

"Mine, too."

"Americans have pampered feet."

"Pampered lives."

"The whole system is corrupt."

"Rotting and dying."

They smiled at each other. "C'mon, lazy boy," Maud said. "Race ya."

They reached the cathedral at the same time and cooled in its shade. Jeff planted his hands on his hips and stared at the huge, green-domed building.

"Power and money," he muttered.

"Lucy used to say that they build them so big to make us feel small."

"We have to change it."

Maud knelt and retied a sneaker. "No way you can change that," she said, and tipped her head toward the church. "Or that." She pointed downhill at the capitol.

She rose and brushed her hands on her thighs, then stepped toward the curb. "Let's just worry about getting to the college." As soon as her thumb was out, a car pulled over. Jeff waved it away and yanked Maud back a step.

"Why'd you do that?"

"I don't want to ride in a Mercedes."

She rolled her eyes and stuck out her thumb again. A new Volkswagen bus pulled over. "This okay?"

He smiled. "Perfect. Let's go."

The van door slid open. Maud smiled, stepped forward, then paused. The van, which had been stripped of all seats but the front two, was packed with people. She turned and whispered to Jeff, "We should have taken the Mercedes. Serves you right if you have to sit on a guy's lap."

Two bearded men wiggled over and made room.

Jeff avoided laps, but was sitting with his knees rammed under his chin.

"Thanks for the lift," Maud said. "Were you all at the rally?"

"We missed it," said a woman seated directly across from Maud. "We didn't buy a map, we got lost, and we missed it."

"Where are you going," the driver shouted, "and how do we get there?"

Maud and Jeff laughed, but they were the only ones. "Straight up this street about three miles," Maud said. "Are you going that far?"

"Why not?!" the driver said, and they veered back into traffic. Car horns honked. Maud chewed on her lip.

Lucy had loved to hitchhike, both because it flouted family rules and because she claimed she met the most interesting people. "If they're not dangerous, they're fascinating," she had counseled her younger sister.

"Are you all together?" Maud asked.

"Good question!" someone in the far back of the van shouted, provoking laughter from the others.

"We certainly are," a man next to Jeff said. "Physically, politically, and spiritually together."

Everyone laughed again, and Maud looked them over. They didn't seem dangerous. But then, she'd seen pictures of the Manson gang, and they hadn't, either. These people were all pretty young, most wore bandannas or baseball caps, and all the men had beards. She noticed then that Jeff was absently rubbing his chin; perhaps he'd just observed the same thing. She tapped his shoulder. "Mercedes," she whispered. He didn't smile.

"Is the place we're taking you near a K mart or some store like that?" the woman across from Maud asked.

"Pretty close."

Maud was nearly rocked by the happy cheer that erupted.

"We're shopping for shovels," the woman explained. Her companions nodded seriously. "If we don't get the shovels, this trip will be a total loss."

"Carolyn, how can you possibly make that judgment now?" the man seated on Maud's right said. "The trip is not yet over." Others concurred.

"Where are you all from?" Jeff asked. And do you know anyone named Manson? Maud added silently.

"Utopia!" the driver shouted, and the others either cheered or laughed.

Carolyn adjusted the Chicago Cubs cap on her head. "We're from near a town up north called Grand River." She waited for acknowledgment. Maud nodded. "We've started a commune. We've been there since early April."

"And we should be there now," one of the men said. "We have too much work to do to have given up a whole day for the march."

Carolyn tugged again on her cap. "Maybe that's true, Peter, but a majority of the group voted to come." She turned to Maud and Jeff. "When we vote to do something, we all support the decision."

"I can support a decision," Peter said, "and still believe it a mistake."

"Do you think that's possible," someone else asked, "in a philosophical sense?"

"Of course."

"Absolutely not."

They were off and running, ten voices debating a point. Maud saw that Jeff was following the argument with wide eyes and a smile. She leaned back and looked out the van window, thinking that if she didn't watch, they might make a wrong turn and she'd be driven off in a van full of hippies.

There were rising voices, and laughter, and twice two women in the back retorted a point by breaking into song. A bean bag appeared and sailed the length of the van. Jeff leaned forward, pulled into the debate. Maud leaned against him. Although the discussion didn't engage her, the good spirits did. The mood was so unlike the rabid anger they had encountered when escaping the rally. Suddenly, the bean bag flew into her lap. Maud tossed it twice between her hands, then sent it flying across heads.

Jeff slipped in a question. "There are ten of you living together?"

"Twenty-four," said Carolyn. "The others came in different cars."

"We lost them in a town called Fridley," the driver said.

Jeff leaned back. "Twenty-four! Together? Sharing, uh, everything?"

"Whoa!" Carolyn said. "I share work and property

170

with everyone, but I sleep with him," and she banged the back of the driver's seat. "My husband." The driver tipped his White Sox baseball cap.

Jeff flushed. "I meant . . . you *own* things together?"

"Thirty acres," someone said, "four vehicles, a decrepit farmhouse —"

"We're building a dorm," Carolyn interjected.

"Five hundred feet of sandy lakeshore and some equipment," the man continued.

But no shovels, thought Maud.

"Who's in charge?"

Again, everyone but Maud and Jeff laughed. "No one," said Carolyn. "And everyone. We make decisions after lots of talk." She leaned toward Jeff. "What we're creating is a community that is organically different from this one." She gestured toward the outside, where the broad street was lined with huge lawns and large houses. The others murmured agreement. "It works," she said firmly.

Worked since April, added Maud silently. One month. She sighed and looked at her hands. Quit being so cynical, she commanded herself.

Jeff tapped his fingertips against his knee. "I can't really imagine anything so different. How did you decide to do it? How do you function now? How . . ." He furrowed his brow, stumped. "What's it like?"

"Long version or short?"

"Short," said Maud. "The next corner is where we need to get out."

"It's nice," Carolyn said. The others nodded.

The van veered and pulled alongside the curb. "Is this the corner? Did I hear that?" the driver asked.

"This is it," said Maud. She nearly fell backward out of the van when the door slid open. Jeff grabbed her hand and held on.

"Which way to K mart?" the driver asked.

Maud pointed. "Turn here, then straight up the street about a mile. It will be on your left. After you get the shovels, keep on going up the street and watch for signs for Highway Ten. It will connect with the highway going north. It does that somewhere around Fridley."

Ten people groaned.

"Thanks so much," Jeff called.

"Come and visit," someone said.

"Come and stay," said someone else. The door was slammed shut, and the van careered back into traffic.

"Hope they make it," said Maud.

"Yeah," Jeff said. "I hope they do."

"Ice cream," said Jeff, "is the perfect food. Terrific taste, and no animals died." He scooped another large spoonful from his bowl. Syrup pooled at the bowl's rim, and Maud tensed. Eighteen, and for the first time in her life she was eating in the living room. Sitting on the Oriental rug and eating. Don't spill, please don't spill, she felt compelled to say.

Instead: "My mother used to go nuts about getting food on this rug. We were absolutely never allowed to eat in here."

Jeff licked a dribble of chocolate syrup off his lip.

"Do you suppose that's why Lucy rebelled and became a revolutionary? Maybe she had too many years of hearing 'Don't eat on the rug.' "

Maud smiled. "Probably."

"Do you miss her?"

Maud stared at him. Of course she missed Lucy. Why even ask?

"I meant your mother."

Oh. Different. Still . . . "Of course I miss my mother."

"Was she like you?"

"No!"

His eyebrows shot up.

"She was . . . not like me." Elegant. Sure. Graceful. "She was an artist."

"So are you. That quilt you showed me when we got back was terrific."

"I'm a craftsman. No, craftswoman. Whatever. Whether I'm doing a garden or a quilt, I make a plan, I find a tool, and I do it. My mother was always observing, then interpreting in acrylic or watercolor. I just make things."

"I'm not sure there's a difference."

"Big difference."

"Wanna fight over it?"

"No."

"I don't miss my dad," he said cheerfully. "Of course, he's not dead. But he's gone as good as dead."

"You could find him."

"I could. But it's like . . . that part of my life is over. Like being five. I'm never going to be five again, so I won't waste tears over it. It's done. Dad was part of my childhood, but now childhood's over. Speaking of dads, where's yours?"

"I'm sure he's here. Probably up in his study. When he gets going on some writing I might not see him for days, but I know he's home because I hear these soft noises from the third floor."

"Like a ghost."

Maud concentrated on her empty ice-cream bowl. How true. She lived with ghosts. "Sort of."

Jeff stretched out his long legs and prodded her gently with a foot. "So, do you still want to sleep with me in a tent?"

"What?"

"That's what you said. During the rally you practically jumped into my lap, gave me this hot look, and said, 'I want to sleep with you in a tent.' "

"I did?" She was blushing. A whole-body blush.

"I'd like to go camping," he continued. "I'm probably the only native Minnesotan who's never done it, I guess because my mom has always liked to vacation within sight of a bar and a restaurant. I'd like to try it. Would, um, you go?"

"You mean now? This weekend?"

"No. I promised I'd be back tonight. But sometime."

She cupped her bowl in her hands. "Great."

"Would you . . ." he cupped his own bowl. He was avoiding looking at her. "I mean, say we go camping together. Would you tell your father, tell him that you're going with me? Going with a guy?"

Good question. "No," she said slowly. "Not because it's you, but because it's with a guy. I suppose I'd lie to him."

"Yeah. Me, too."

"Dumb, huh?"

"I guess. But I have so many arguments with the world that I try to avoid them with my mother."

"That's wise."

"So let's do it. Let's do it and lie."

"I'm willing."

"I mean, I'm not saying we have to share a bag together, or anything. You know?"

"I know what you mean, Jeff."

He sat back. "Actually, I don't have a sleeping bag. I'll get one."

"Don't. I bought a new one last year. I have two." And they can be zipped together, she thought. "My whole family used to camp pretty often, and I have everything."

"Far out. God, I've always hated that expression."

"When should we go?" Don't push him. Guys hate pushing.

"When it's warmer, maybe. Three weeks?"

Maud calculated. "That's prom."

"Sorry. Maybe . . ."

"It would be perfect — camping instead of prom."

He smiled. "I can't believe it. I've made a date for prom." He shifted, crawled to where she was sitting on the rug, then kissed her and sealed the promise.

175

· 6 ·

"I can't go camping."

Maud took a breath, then gently kicked the rolled-up sleeping bag lying at her feet.

"I'm sorry to tell you on such short notice," said Jeff. "But my stepfather is having an operation tomorrow."

"That's awful. What's wrong?"

"Hernia. So it's not major, not like they're going after cancer. But they are going to knock him out, and Mom wants me to hold her hand."

"Of course."

"I really feel bad about this. Let's set another date right now."

They agreed to meet at a state park in two weeks, the day after his graduation ceremony.

"A perfect way to celebrate," Jeff said.

"And it will be warmer," added Maud.

Maud's father was sympathetic about the canceled trip. "That's too bad," he said. "I hope Natalie feels better soon."

Maud swallowed. She'd almost forgotten she'd lied about her camping companion. Edgy from the disappointment, she practically snarled. "Actually, Dad, it was Jeff that canceled. I was going with him, not Natalie. You might as well know."

So there. He knows.

Mr. Dougherty slid off the kitchen stool, looked about for something to do, decided to refill his coffee mug.

Say it, Dad, she silently challenged. Say it's sinful. Say you forbid it. Or, maybe, say you think it's wonderful, an expression of the new freedom. Say it. Find the words, Poet.

He sipped coffee. "I'm not sure, Maud," he said at last in a soft, rich voice, his poet's reading voice, "that it's wise to be so deeply involved when you're so young." He turned and emptied his coffee. "But maybe it doesn't matter. There seem to be no more rules. The rules have all been broken."

Broken rules were discussed Saturday night in their living room. To Maud's surprise, her father had invited friends over. "I thought you'd be gone," he said.

"You never throw parties. I think it's great. Playing poker?"

"All writers. We'll be reading from our works in progress."

"Whoa. Hope the neighbors don't call the cops."

Maud greeted each of the guests, then retreated to her room. When she emerged to fix a snack, she caught fragments of conversation. As the guests ate in the living room on the hundred-year-old rug, they discussed the breakdown of rules. Evidently her father had told them all of her camping plans. She'd kill him.

But first, listen.

As she had done as a young child whenever her parents had guests, she sat on the steps and eavesdropped. The six writers were eager to discuss what one of them called the moral disintegration of the nation.

"Appalling . . ." A glass clinked against wood.

"Given the lies from our elected leaders . . ." Silk rustled against upholstery.

"Women are entitled . . ." Fingers rummaged through a cracker basket.

Nothing louder than a cough. Even at their angriest, they spoke with a dispassionate civility. Maud knew them all, had known some of them most of her life. She knew their work, knew their children, their voting patterns. She didn't doubt that they were outraged by the war, by the shooting of protesters, the riots, the children armed with bombs. But it hadn't seemed to rouse any of them. She could almost hear Lucy's scorn, see her sister pointing an accusing finger at what she'd call the bourgeois somnolence.

Maud was also guilty. Too often she had felt as if she were sleepwalking in a tempest. Even during the rare times when she was alert and involved, like at the parade in Red Cedar or when at the center, she'd only felt so much like a big black bird circling and circling far above the world, trying to spot something moving, something shiny and bright that would compel her to dive down and grab hold.

Jeff canceled again. "I started work, and right away we had three days of rain, and now the boss wants me to work on Saturday. There are a lot of billboards that need paint."

Excuses. She hated excuses. Just tell the truth. "Jeff, if you're having second thoughts, I understand. We could do something else."

"I want to go camping," he said firmly, "but I can't blow off work. Mom has been making noises about the college tuition bill. She and I have this deal about who pays how much, and I need to come up with my share. I'm lucky she'll pay anything. She never went to college and doesn't really see the need. It's complicated. I'll write and try to explain. And I do want to go camping. I mean it."

He must have written immediately after ending the phone call because the next day, when Maud arrived home from work, there was a fat letter from Jeff. In it, he apologized again and then dove into sharing everything on his mind. Maud replied with her own fat letter. He wrote back, then wrote again without waiting for an answer. He wrote beautiful letters. On plain white paper, in small, clear handwriting, he bared his soul and probed hers. Reading the letters, Maud often thought of her mother. "Don't ever fall for a poet," she had occasionally warned Maud, but always with a laugh, as if she knew how sweet such a seduction could be.

Though the letters were overflowing in thought and emotion, they were spare in facts. And one July morning, with the camping trip still ahead of them, Maud scanned the morning paper, spotted the list of draft lottery numbers that had been drawn the previous

179

night, and realized that, though she knew what books Jeff had beside his bed, she didn't know his birth date. Since student deferments had been abolished, any boy who turned nineteen in 1970 was up for grabs. If you were born on the wrong day, Uncle Sam had a claim. The war needed fresh bodies.

She found Keller's birthday on the list. October 21, draft number five. "Damn," she muttered. Poor Keller.

But maybe not. His father was an attorney with a large Kansas company and had connections everywhere. No, Keller's Harvard education probably wouldn't be interrupted by something like the draft.

She wondered if Jeff had family connections. What people could a meatpacker's kid know? Any contacts with power? Maud wished, then, that she had the habit of prayer. She wanted to pray for all the boys with unlucky birthdays.

When she returned from the center that afternoon, Jeff and Gumbo were sitting on the back steps. She stifled a squeal, allowed a smile, and hugged them both.

Gumbo gave her a broad grin. "We're running away."

Jeff didn't smile. "I apologize for just showing up."

Maud sat on the bottom step. That afternoon, Crawford had blown juice out of his straw onto Maud and she was sticky. Then she'd been caught behind a bus on her bicycle, and she was coated with diesel exhaust. She was glad to see the boys, but she wanted most to shower.

Gumbo sniffed. "This might be sort of rude, but . . . is that incense?"

"It's sweat, diesel, and apple juice."

"Wow. Hard day, huh?"

"Not as hard as yours, I bet. What are your numbers?" Not good ones, she was certain. After all, Gumbo had said they were running away.

"Three sixty-two," Jeff said glumly.

Maud shrieked, then covered her mouth. "Jeff, that's great! It said in the paper that no one over two hundred would get drafted. That's practically the last number!"

"Mine's six," chirped Gumbo.

Suddenly, Maud felt as if she'd actually been hit by the bus. She exhaled and reached up to hug Gumbo. "I'm sorry. I'm so sorry." She looked at Jeff. Of course he was bummed out, probably hurting more for his friend than he would for himself.

Maud knew then that she loved him. After only two demonstrations, one night together, and no dates, she loved him.

"Where are you running to?" she asked.

"That's sort of exaggerating," said Gumbo. "We thought we'd go camping. We thought maybe it would be cool to spend a weekend in the middle of America the Beautiful so we can appreciate what I'll be defending. But we don't have any equipment. Jeff thought you might loan us stuff."

"I've got everything," said Maud. "You're welcome to use it."

"Come with us," said Gumbo. "It might cheer him up. I haven't been able to."

Maud was mystified. "Aren't you feeling awful? I'd be dying."

"Sure I feel awful. But what happens, happens. Try telling that to him."

"You'll get killed," Jeff said. "You're like a baby sometimes, and you'll get over there and just walk smiling into trouble."

"Thanks, man, for your confidence. Do you see," he said to Maud, "why I want you along? My friend just ain't a whole lotta fun."

"Please come," said Jeff.

Camping with two boys. No chaperone. Maud shrugged. "Sure," she said. "Sounds like a whole lotta fun."

It was exhausting. During the two days they were gone, any number of things both amused and frustrated Maud: the boys' halting and uncertain efforts to pitch tents and build fires, their dismay about the trail food, their boisterous water games when swimming. Like camping with preschoolers, she decided.

They had brought two tents. The first night, after watching the fire burn low, Gumbo had gone to one. Jeff followed Maud to the other. "So...um..." was all he could say.

"So, um, do I want to zip our bags together?"

He exhaled. "Yes."

"Did you bring anything?"

"Huh?"

Maud smiled. Sometimes his usually wonderful

voice reminded her of a seal's. She took his arm and led him back to the fire. She added a log, and they sat. When the log caught heat from the embers, she spoke.

"Once upon a time," Maud said, "there was this girl who was really screwed up by all the things going on in her life. Her sister had just died, and all around her the world seemed to be going crazy."

Jeff nestled closer.

"This girl was really a strong person. She could do things, Jeff. Great things like portage a canoe for a mile, or fix windows, or bake a pie —"

"You bake pies?"

"The best. But this is a story, so hush. Anyway, this girl had pretty much stopped doing things. She was just muddling through day by day, just bouncing off other people's lives. And there was this guy. And because he smelled nice and had once held her sister, or maybe because she didn't have the energy to turn around and walk away" — Maud sighed — "she let him."

"Let him?"

"You know what I mean. And besides hating herself because it was so awful and stupid, the worst thing was for weeks she worried she might be pregnant."

"Was she?"

"No. But worrying about it was a nightmare, and she vowed never again. Never again with a jerk, and never again risk getting pregnant."

Shadowed, his face was almost handsome. "I'm not sure," he said finally, "what the most interesting thing about that story is."

"I think I'd like to, Jeff. I mean, these days, it's no big deal, right? But did you bring anything?"

"Rubbers? No." A sad smile slid over his face. "But I know where to get some. Next time?"

"Next time."

The next weekend they camped again, without Gumbo. Jeff came prepared, and this time they zipped their bags together.

On the anniversary of Lucy's death, Maud and her father went to Iowa to visit the Amana colonies and to look at quilts. It seemed the most peaceful thing to do.

"But mostly," she explained to Jeff in a phone call prior to leaving, "we just want to be gone. There will probably be lots of 'One Year After' news stories that we'd just as soon miss."

At her father's suggestion she invited Jeff along, but he and his mother had their own sad anniversary to observe and were spending it fishing on the Mississippi. Maud thought it interesting that both deaths, Lucy's and Tom's, had happened in the same week. During the same week in August 1969, she and Jeff — miles apart, without knowledge of each other — had experienced similar volcanic eruptions, then suffered the same rocky slide. And when they landed, they had tumbled down together.

A week after returning from Iowa, Maud was reading the newspaper at breakfast. "Where's the box?" she asked.

"What box?" said her father.

"The casualty box, the thing where they list the weekly death toll."

"Now that you mention it, I don't think I've seen it for some time."

"Aren't they still dying? Have our brilliant generals managed to turn Vietnam into a war without any dead people?"

Mr. Dougherty crisply refolded his section of the newspaper while looking at Maud with raised eyebrows, his "You sound like Lucy" look. "Instead of sitting in your pajamas and spitting sarcasm at your father, why don't you call the paper and get an answer?" he said.

"Maybe I will."

"I hope you do. I'm going to the grocery store. We need coffee."

After double-checking the entire paper for the casualty count, Maud did call and spoke with an editor.

"We dropped it months ago," he said.

"Have the soldiers stopped dying?"

"The numbers are pretty low. Hardly go over fifty each week."

"Fifty dead? Fifty? That's a lot."

"Not like the old days, young lady, not like when there'd be a hundred or more. But they've curtailed the ground war and the bombings, you know. Hell, there aren't even any peace talks or demonstrations to report. News-wise, the war isn't much of a story anymore."

Maud began searching the morning paper every

day for war stories and almost always found them buried inside. The front page had been handed over to other things: turmoil in the Mideast, student violence in Europe, race relations, women's lib demonstrations, drugs, and venereal disease. It was as if the great floodwaters of the war had receded, exposing a wasted land.

"Soldiers are still dying," she exclaimed to Jeff one night as they huddled by their campfire. Camping was their weekly ritual, one often shared with Gumbo. On this trip, however, they were alone, celebrating — or maybe lamenting — Jeff's departure for college. All day he had been bursting with anxiety, wanting to talk about the impending change. What could she tell him about dorm life? Did she know anyone going to St. Cloud? Were all professors as decent as her father? Would she send him cookies? Maud, sympathetic, had restrained her anger over the disappearance of the war news until they were sitting by the fire. She could hold it in no longer.

Jeff held her hand. "Well, Nixon's brought home some troops, and fewer guys are dying. Maybe that's why."

"Does that matter? Has it suddenly become a moral war because only half as many men are dying each week? They're *still* dying. Our side, their side. Three months ago it seemed like the whole country was going to explode. Now it's nothing. Have you seen *Life* magazine this week? The biggest news is baseball and the new TV shows!"

He laced his fingers through hers. He let her talk.

"Guys are still getting drafted, still getting killed. They say it's not news. It's like suddenly everyone's trying to forget something that's still happening."

"They won."

"What do you mean? It hasn't been won, they're not even having peace talks. No one has won anything, Jeffrey."

"The bastards in the White House have won. They've worn us out, and they get to keep their war. No one's watching any longer. I'm guilty, too. Once upon a time I shouted and marched and wrote my goddamn congressman. But now . . . I have to admit that what most concerns me is if I'll have enough money for textbooks and whether I'll ever be able to sneak you into the dorm for a night." He stretched out a long leg and prodded a fallen log back into the fire. "Of course people still care, Maud. Maybe it's just that no one knows what to do."

Maud found something to do. The next week, while Jeff and her old high school friends settled into dorms and freshman English, and as her father resettled into his routine of teaching, Maud spent her free time at the library hunting through folk music books and records until she had a collection of songs about peace. She taught them to herself, then taught them to her preschoolers. After two weeks of rehearsals, they gave a concert for the senior citizens at the center, then went on tour, visiting the area nursing homes. For each stop she prepared flyers that urged people to write their congressman and demand he vote against military funding. The flyers also listed the names and ages of the previous week's war dead, information Maud got with a regular call to the newspaper editor. After her second request for the names, the editor said, "What the hell — you're right, sweetheart," and resumed publishing the weekly list.

In between concerts with the children, Maud immersed herself in the routine at the center. She taught the seniors macramé and learned from them the rules of whist. And every day she eagerly anticipated the arrival of the children, welcoming the explosion of noise and movement and smell. She played, taught them letters and numbers, and was herself instructed on the names of dinosaurs.

"It's all I want," she confessed to Jeff on a chilly October night as they sat by their campfire on a bluff overlooking the Saint Croix River. "Meaningful work and something to do on a Saturday night."

She thought he'd laugh, but when she looked, she saw only a deep gloom.

"What's wrong?"

"I wish what I was doing were meaningful. It's a waste."

"I thought you liked it."

"It's stupid. Stupid papers and stupid arguments. My philosophy professor can lecture for an hour and say nothing. What's the point of sitting and listening to him? He goes on and on about economic inequities in the world, or he talks about the war and its origins. Meanwhile, everything continues. People just talk. God, I admire what you've been doing — you actually got a major newspaper to admit it was wrong and do something. Most people are just satisfied to talk, as if that's action. No wonder your sister got so angry. I can sort of understand her. Understand how you can get to a point where you feel so hopeless about the possibilities that you want to blow everything up."

Maud pulled her sweater cuffs down and tucked her hands under her armpits. "She failed, Jeff. She didn't blow *everything* up, she blew *herself* up. That's all."

She felt him kiss the top of her head.

"Maybe those people had the right idea," he said.

"What people?"

"The ones we met the day of the march, from that commune. Instead of banging heads against society's brick wall, they moved off to build a totally new society. They couldn't change the world, so they decided to change the way *they* lived."

"Dropped out."

"I don't think so. Dropping out is more like what Gumbo's doing. He just sleeps and reads. He doesn't even go out of the house to buy drugs. He's been straight for weeks now." Jeff sighed deeply; Maud, sitting close beside him, moved as he moved. "Maybe I'm just worried about him. Maybe I'm just down on everything because I know my best friend doesn't have much time left. He'll be called up soon. It will kill him, Maud. One way or another, the army will kill him. He doesn't seem to care. Says it will all take care of itself. Not caring — that's dropping out."

A gust of chilly wind hit them. Maud rose. "I'm

going inside the tent to get warm." Jeff didn't move. "Do you want to come? I'll tell you a bedtime story." He shook his head slightly.

Maud was torn. Should she freeze and keep him company or get warm and leave him alone with his demons?

No contest. After all, she was in love. Maud sat beside him, took his hand, and together they watched the moon climb slowly into the sky.

· 7 ·

Maud canceled their next camping trip. "The seniors have decided to put on a play," she explained to Jeff during their regular Wednesday-night call. "Can you believe it? They want to do *Harvey* because it has so many old people's parts. I said I'd help with sets and costumes, and the first production meeting is this weekend."

"That's okay. I'll survive. Maybe I'll go by myself."

"You won't survive that; they're predicting frost."

On Sunday night she called to see if he had actually gone camping by himself. He wasn't there.

"Gone all weekend," his roommate said. "Don't know where. Still hasn't come back."

She tried again on Monday and Tuesday. Finally, on Wednesday night he answered.

"I was going to call you. Guess where I was?"

"Chicago? Chasing bunnies at the Playboy Club?"

"Woodlands."

"Where's that? What's that?"

"The commune up north. Friday afternoon I figured I couldn't handle a weekend of football and keggers, so I drove to Grand River and asked around for the commune. I thought someone would know. I finally

191

found it. I drove in at about ten at night, thinking it was the craziest thing I'd ever done — and they were really glad to see me. They remembered. And they asked about you. Maud, it was incredible. It was so nice. I cut wood, I hauled lumber, I didn't want to leave."

"I didn't know you could be excited by manual labor!"

"Action excites me. Doing something. Actually doing something. Maud, it was so warm there. I mean, spiritually, you know? These people share the land, and they share a future, and they . . ."

It was a monologue, and she listened. At first, she was moved by his fervor, then — suddenly, miserably — felt cut adrift, left to sink slowly, just as she might feel had he been telling her about a bright and beautiful lab partner.

"They said we're welcome to come there and camp. Anytime. Let's go next weekend."

"I have the play."

"What? But not every weekend, right?"

"I made a commitment."

"Every darn weekend? I want you to see the commune, Maud. You can give me one little weekend, can't you?"

"Aren't you the one who preaches about commitments? I sure have heard it somewhere, and I think from someone I sleep with."

They fought. She shouted, he yelled, they both called names. By the time they cooled down and said good night, her father had risen from his desk, alarmed, and everyone on Jeff's dorm floor was listening at a door.

Every weekend Jeff went north, and every weekend Maud immersed herself in the paint and wood and fabric of the show. She bought four tickets to opening night. Jeff had promised to attend, and she hoped her father would consider finding a date.

The play was canceled. Two days before opening night, one of the cast members, Ida, broke her hip when she fell while chasing her cat down her apartment steps. She had an understudy, but that woman had had a minor stroke two weeks before, and now she mingled lines from all the parts.

Maud left a message for Jeff with his roommate, told her father to forget about finding a date, and pinned the tickets to her bulletin board. On what should have been opening night, she and Natalie took flowers to the hospital and held Ida's hand. They listened as she recited her lines to a roomful of visitors.

"Next spring," Maud reassured Ida as her listeners applauded her final line. "We'll do the show next spring. Everything's ready."

She drove Natalie to her dorm.

"It's too bad Jeff didn't come down anyway," said Natalie. "I'd like to have seen him. The last time I saw him he was knocked out and bloody."

"Now he doesn't even have any scars."

"We all have scars."

"That's deep. Listen to that music! Did someone's volume control get stuck?"

"Probably a party. But then, there's always a party. Why don't you come in and we'll find it?"

"Nat, I haven't been to a party in months." She made a quick mental count. "Over a year."

"It's time. Have a beer, dance with a stranger — it'll do you good."

"Maybe a beer, but no dancing."

Natalie's room was on the fourth floor of an older dorm. Halfway up the stairwell they met three girls. One of them was vomiting.

"Bad dope," one of her friends said, "mixed with too much beer."

"She's really sick," the other added.

"She lives on my hall," Natalie said to Maud. They helped the girl to her room. Maud found a bucket in the lavatory and brought it to the room. The girl was sleeping.

"I think she's okay," Natalie said to the girl's roommate.

The roommate shrugged. "Happens all the time. I'm going out for coffee."

Natalie sighed. "I never should have let my parents blackmail me into staying in the dorm. Living with freshmen is hell; I play mother so often. I know this girl's boyfriend. I'll go see if he wants to keep her company."

While Natalie searched for the boyfriend, Maud stood watch in the room. She had never liked to drink, and since summer, when she began spending so much time with Jeff, she had smoked pot only once, a ceremonial joint lit with some old high school friends the night before they headed east for college.

As she watched the girl's shoulders move slightly, Maud inhaled deeply and was suddenly sickened by the stench of vomit. She vowed then never again to drink or smoke. "I will be pure," she promised herself.

She rose from her chair and browsed through the stacks of books on the two desks. *Slavery and Empire. Origins of the Russian Revolution.* Austen, Fitzgerald, Dickens, and Woolf. All subjects and authors she'd once looked forward to studying.

The door opened, and a boy poked his head in. "Stones marathon in the lounge. Starts at ten."

Maud waved him away and smiled, suddenly recognizing the truth of college life: it was one long beach party, with discussion topics.

She wanted out. She had to get out. The vomit, the noise, the music, the dope, the beer, the big fat storybooks. Out Now. "Forgive me, Nat," she whispered, "but I'm leaving."

She scribbled a note and left it on the sleeping body, then raced down the stinky stairwell and burst into the delicious, cold December air. Snow was falling, and it soothed her as quickly as a massage. She whistled as she walked toward her car.

There was a small group of students clustered in the parking lot.

"Kierkegaard is full of . . ."

"Niebuhr had it, man, when he said . . ."

Marx and Hegel and Dostoyevsky and Larry and Moe. The joints flew as fast as the words.

"Shut up," she wanted to say. "Just shut up and go plant a garden." Okay, she conceded, it was December in Minnesota. Forget the garden, but go paint a picture or throw a pot or teach a kid to do a cartwheel. Just shut up and do something.

She drove away quickly, hurled forward by the crushing urge to get away from the college, away from the lights and music and smell, from the clamor of cracking bright minds. She was certain, and it was a cleansing revelation, that there was nothing there for her.

"Hello-ho, Maud!"

Before she could speak, Maud had to make a conscious effort to return her jaw to its normal position. As she did, she walked with the telephone toward the kitchen, hoping to maximize the distance from her father, who was watching television in the den. She breathed deeply.

"Hi, Mrs. Sanborn."

"For Pete's sake, call me Connie. Just because that son of mine hasn't brought you home yet doesn't mean we can't be friends."

"I *was* going to come at Thanksgiving."

"I know, I know, but I was in Vegas. Sorry. With Tommy gone, I just couldn't face stuffing a turkey."

"I understand."

"Of course you do. Holidays aren't real fun with

dead family, are they? Betcha wondering why I'm calling."

Betcha right. Boyfriend's mother rings up at nearly
ten? Major mystery. "Well . . ." said Maud.

"Is Jeff there?"

"No."

"Do you know where he might be? I had some news
I just had to tell him, so I called his room and his
roommate said he'd *moved* out and *dropped* out yesterday."

"What?!"

"That's pretty much what *I* said. Well, it had four
letters anyway. That Gilbert — or Hobart, whoever
— said Jeff had officially dropped his classes, quit his
campus job, and split. With no message. Not a word
about where he was going. He sure as hell didn't come
home."

Oh God. Headed north, that's where. "I'm sure he
went to Woodlands. The commune."

"The *what?*"

"You didn't know? It's this place up north he's been
visiting since fall. A commune. It's a bunch of people
who share —"

"Oh, honey, I sure know what a commune is."

"But it's not what you might think. It's not . . . he
said it's not . . . anything wild."

Jeff's mom chuckled. "I'm sure it isn't. I know my
boy, and if he's involved, the place has gotta be tamer
than a Moose lodge. Oh, hon, do you really think
that's where he went?"

"I'd bet on it. It's kind of a puzzle, though, because

197

I talked to him two nights ago and he said nothing." And he must have known what he was going to do, she added to herself.

"Same here. Talked on Sunday. A commune. Well, I think I'm gonna have to go fix a highball and muddle this over. Maybe it makes sense."

"Maybe."

"Holy Mother, I'd better fix a double."

"Mrs. Sanborn —"

"Connie, Connie, Connie."

"— he'll probably call or write to me eventually. And I think I have the address; he put it in an old letter. I could dig that up if you want to hold on."

"Save his letters, do you? No, I'll just wait for him to tell me what he wants to tell me. But if he contacts you first, tell him to call his mother, pronto."

"I'll write to him tonight. What news was it you had for him? I could pass it on."

"I almost forgot. Do you know his friend Gumbo? Of course you do, all that camping last summer. Hmm, not sure what I think about that. Anyway, he's gone."

"Gone?"

"Canada. He left a note on the fridge for his folks. They got in from work tonight and found it. Took five hundred bucks from his pop's underwear drawer and drove off in his mother's car. They're hopping mad. Fred, his dad, was in the army in the big war. Fought in the Battle of the Bulge." She chuckled. "Still fighting it. The fellow's gotta weigh two-fifty."

Maud reeled. Gumbo. Sweet, placid, harmless

Gumbo. A draft evader. Forever a fugitive. What happens, happens, he'd said. Maud swallowed. "I'll write Jeff tonight."

"Shocker, huh? I think it's fine. I mean, my Tommy is dead, and for what? Some choice we've given these boys: kill or run. What the hell — Canada or a commune. No difference there."

"Jeff can come home."

"And he damn well better, and he'd better bring you. Honey, I'm sorry to bother you so late. It was a little hard finding the right number. I knew your name, he'd told me that much. I tried two Doughertys before I got the right one."

"I'm really glad you called."

"I'll sleep better now that I've talked to you. What a day! And now it looks like we've got a blizzard. Snowing up there?"

"Seven inches since noon."

"Same here. December in Minnesota can be a bitch. Take care, hon."

Maud went to her room and rummaged through her desk until she found the letter Jeff had written from the commune. His usual pattern had been to wait until he was back in his Spartan dorm room before writing, but for some reason during one trip he had been impatient to share with her what he was seeing and doing. He had sounded so happy.

Dear Maud,

This is so rare: I'm alone here . . . absolutely alone. It's a fantastic afternoon — cloudless

*sky and it's almost sixty-five. And it's Novem-
ber IN MINNESOTA! Anyway, there's a
meeting going on here, something about the
budget, and the group got inspired to meet
down on the beach. I didn't go along because I
don't really belong so I didn't think I should
vote on anything and also I knew that if I was
sitting there in the middle of a discussion
there'd be no way — none — I could keep my
mouth shut. So I stayed behind. I've got Blind
Faith playing on the group's stereo, a bowl of
fresh apple crisp, and a cardinal on the tree
outside the window.*

You should be here, then it would be perfect.

*As much as I like everyone, it is nice to be
alone. It never fails to amaze me how twenty-
four people can manage to get along day after
day. Yeah, sure, there is some disagreement
and snipping, but generally speaking, they
make it work. The quiet is nice, though.*

*They finished a building today, the second
one they've put up. Remember when we met
them after the peace march and they only had
an old farmhouse? Well, besides the new building, which is sort of a garage-workshed thing,
there is a dorm with showers and a kitchen —
that's where I am now. It's a big beautiful
kitchen with a great window looking right into
the woods.*

*A few people still sleep in the old farmhouse,
but it leaks. It's loaded with antiques, though.*

Or was loaded. Last week an antiques dealer from Chicago drove up and bought a van full of stuff. Nine thousand dollars' worth. The old farmer who sold the place to the group used to watch TV sitting in an eight-hundred-dollar chair!

You asked me once how they could afford prime Minnesota lakeshore and forest property. Now I know. When I was hauling wood today, I asked one of the guys. He said they all pitched in what they could. One or two people had a lot, I gathered. Somebody's rich grandpa died, and somebody else was loaded, and the others did what they could with savings or cars they sold. The property cost about thirty thou, and they have sort of a mortgage with the farmer. Oh, this is wild — the farmer is eighty and he moved in with his seventy-year-old girlfriend. Can you believe it? I guess kids aren't the only ones breaking rules.

The cool thing about the money is that no one person swings more power or clout just cuz he put in ten thou instead of five hundred. Everybody's valued — as long as he does his share of the work.

They need you. The garden was a bust. No one really knew much about gardening and now all they have for a crop is zucchini and tomatoes. Thanks to the antique dealer, they won't starve, but self-sufficiency is maybe a distant goal. I like zucchini and tomatoes, es-

pecially if you mix them with rice. Oops, be back.

I'm back. I had to stir the soup. Everyone will be here in about an hour, ready to eat. And then . . . a wild Saturday night. Music, drugs, sex . . .

Just kidding. We'll probably play charades. I told them how my girlfriend was learning to play whist from these old people she knew and everyone was real interested. How many times do I have to tell you that you gotta come visit?

I missed a big celebration last Wednesday. They took the day off from roofing the garage and other work and celebrated their six-month anniversary. Exactly six months since the first van arrived and they began to build their new community. A year ago there were just a few friends hanging around a college apartment talking about the messed-up world. Then they did something. They figured out what they wanted, they organized, they committed.

I'm committed — to hauling and stacking more firewood before I go tomorrow. There's always this job list posted, and people are supposed to find something on it that they're willing to do. The list is drawn up by a central committee that sort of administers things and handles problems. It's elected by everyone. They haven't got the kinks out of their system yet, it's all sort of evolving, but they are trying. What's funny is that I got discussed by the C.C.

(central committee, but you probably figured that out). I was on an agenda! They debated whether I should be required to a. do chores and b. pay for meals.

Decision: a. yes b. no

The guy I was with this afternoon got to talking about how it all began. He said they wanted to build a small good world in the middle of a big bad one. I think that's why there are no kids here — yet. Most of the people are pretty young — twenties — and though there are a number of couples, no one has any kids. Everyone agreed it would be best if no one did until the place was a little more established. Till they were sure they had built that good small place in the middle of a big bad one.

I think they're gonna do it.

But they need a decent garden. Can you feed babies zucchini?

And now, for your enjoyment, a Stream of Consciousness from Jeffrey. Soup smells good. I need to study. How's the play? Your dad would look good in a beard. My stepfather bought a new car. My mom got a promotion — first woman in the history of Porter's Pork to be a shift supervisor! I've lost a few pounds. I saw seven deer this morning. All the physical stuff I've been doing — you should see my muscles. Has the real world blown up yet?

Love, J.

Maud folded the letter and pressed it between her hands. "Not yet," she whispered. Not quite. But maybe when he heard the news about Gumbo, he would feel that it had blown up. She found a pencil and paper and tried to write. Even "Dear Jeff" wouldn't come.

She went back downstairs to the den and slumped in a chair. Her father eyed her, but didn't speak. On the screen, a local news anchor was reporting from Saigon. His big story, straight from the war. After the peace talks had resumed in Paris, the fighting had intensified. Maud couldn't figure the logic, but it had happened. The war was news again. She saw trucks rolling in the background behind the reporter, then the camera cut to helicopters. Then there was film of shelling and rooftops and brilliant explosions. Soon, she knew, there'd be a casualty count. Three for us, fifty of them. More or less.

She pictured Jeff sleeping snugly in the crowded commune dorm. She thought of Gumbo speeding north in his mother's car. As the grim-faced reporter returned to the screen, Maud smiled and sank deeper into the comfortable chair. Her two boys were safe.

· 8 ·

Jeff's disappearance aroused Maud, but it was Gumbo's flight that really concerned her. She wanted answers. Was he now a felon? Would he be hunted down? Did he have to hide in Canada? Would she ever see him again?

Though she wasn't scheduled to work, she hurried to the center the next morning, certain someone there would have answers. She burst into the director's office.

"George, what can you tell me about —"

He waved an arm to hush her and pointed at the phone receiver clamped to his ear. Maud sat in a chair. "Just a short staff meeting," he said into the phone. "We won't go over details. Maud's here now. See you in an hour." He hung up the phone and smiled at Maud. "I was about to call you in. There's no emergency, but I have some important news. The paper will have it tomorrow, so I thought it best we meet today. I'm glad you're here now, though. I want to talk privately with you."

Maud narrowed her eyes and looked suspiciously at him. She could feel more bad news coming.

"Our new grant came through, Maud. Last fall a

couple of board members and I decided to try for some private foundation money. Government money is soiled, Maud. We don't think it's right to take government money. That makes us all part of the machine."

"What are you saying, George?"

"The Catherwood Foundation came through most generously." He took a deep breath. "But the nature of the funding is different."

"Say it, George. You're holding something stinky. I can tell."

"As of January first we will no longer offer recreational activities. No senior drama or lunch program or preschool playtime."

Maud rubbed her jaw. Had someone slugged her? "You're kidding."

He shook his head. "The terms of the grant dictate our program."

"Don't give me that, George. I know about grants. You wrote that grant application. You must have asked for it."

"Maud, think of it: we now have money for offices and staff for tenant organizing, and labor organizing, and health education. A nurse, Maud! We can hire a nurse to go out in the streets!"

"She'll find little kids banged up because they had to play in the street, not at the center. And she'll find old people starving because they no longer get even one decent meal. Did you even consult with anyone?"

"One or two board members. Besides, I'm the director. It's my job to give the center direction."

She rose and slammed her fist on the desk. "It's a *community* center, George. That means you ask the *community*."

He tapped his fingertips together and leaned back in his chair. "I know you're attached to your programs, Maud. They've been fun, that's true. But we can use this place to do more. Political action, Maud. That's how to change things, and we have an obligation to change. And we won't dirty ourselves with Nixon's money."

"You once liked spending Nixon's money. You liked thinking if *you* had it he couldn't use it for the war."

"I was wrong. If you cooperate with the enemy, you are the enemy."

Maud sat back down. "Where are they going to go, George? The kids and the seniors — where?"

He lifted, then dropped his hands. "It was time to change, Maud."

Maud left before the staff meeting began. She went home, put on pajamas, and went to bed. After an hour of trying to sleep, she got out of bed and sat at her desk. She was ready to write to Jeff. It was a full letter — full of questions and thoughts about his flight and Gumbo's, the center, the swirling in her soul. She put it all down, then put a coat over her pajamas, boots over bare feet, and walked six blocks over unshoveled sidewalks to mail the letter. She returned home and went back to bed.

She stayed in her pajamas for two days. She watched old movies on television and dusted off and read favorite children's books. Seven times she ate an identical meal: Cheerios and orange juice. Sitting idly in a quiet house, she frequently refigured the answer to a question whose answer she already knew: How long does it take to get a return letter from Grand River, Minnesota?

Too damn long.

On the third night she went downstairs for another bowl of Cheerios and found Jeff sitting in the kitchen with her father, drinking tea. He rose and grinned when she walked in. She froze when she saw him, then turned to her father. "Why didn't you tell me he was here? How long has he been here?"

Mr. Dougherty smiled. "Not long. I would have called you. And I knew eventually you'd put on slippers and shuffle down."

"Dad."

Her father smiled, then fingered a sleeve of the pajamas. "These were your mother's." He nodded to Jeff and left the kitchen.

Maud sighed. His jab about her shuffling in slippers was the closest he'd come in two days to making a comment. The Poet took it all in stride, as if he'd decided long ago he'd let the world have its way with his family. What happens happens.

Maud hugged Jeff. "What are you doing here? Were you at the commune? Have you left the commune? I wrote you there."

"I got the letter."

The television went on in the other room. They heard Maud's father cough and settle into his chair.

"Get dressed, and let's take a walk," Jeff said. He waited in the kitchen while she changed, then they went outside. Maud guided him to a small park at the end of her block.

"Why are you down here? I'm glad to see you, but why?"

"It's only for a night. Can I crash at your house?"

"Of course. Lucy's room. Dad will want you in Lucy's room."

"That's fine. I drove down to sell my car. Tommy's car. I don't need it, and I want to contribute the money to Woodlands. When I got your letter, Maud, I knew I had to talk, not write. You sounded like . . . like I wanted to see you. And I needed to talk to someone about Gumbo. Someone who knows him. Let's sit here." They sat on a bench and huddled together. "When I got your letter yesterday, I shared it with everyone. Well, the parts about Gumbo and the center closing, and how all your people were getting kicked out. Everyone wanted me to tell you how badly they feel, Maud. They sent their love. They all pretty much know about you. Man, I've been sitting in that car for hours." He rose, then lay on the ground and stretched. "This is nice. It's easier to see the stars. I'm actually surprised I can see any, what with all the city lights. I wish I knew the constellations." He patted the snow. "Come on down."

"There's snow. It's cold."

"You're wearing a coat."

"I'll sit on this cozy cast-iron bench, thank you."

"Have you noticed a pattern yet, Maud? About how

209

things are going? Lucy, Tommy, Kent State, the crazy war that will never end, Gumbo thinking he has no choice but to run, your community center that doesn't belong to the community. Power and money, at work." He drew up his knees, pulled his socks over his pants cuffs, stretched his long legs back out on the snow. "I need a ride back to Woodlands, Maud. Would you take me tomorrow?"

"You could take the bus."

"You could drive me. And you could stay for as long as you'd like. We'd put you to work, of course. Will you do it?"

Maud watched the softly falling snow coat her jacket. Lucy and Tommy dead, Gumbo running, the center closed. The things they loved, all gone. She closed her eyes, then was startled when a small snowball hurtled onto her lap and fell apart. She cupped it together and sent it flying back to Jeff. He tossed another. She scooped up a huge handful from the ground and smashed it on his belly.

"Truce!" he called, laughing as he brushed away the snow.

Maud sat back down on the bench. "I'll drive you back tomorrow."

"Will you stay?"

"Is there any privacy? For us, you know . . ."

"The couples seem to manage. But bring your tent."

"It's cold for camping."

"We can zip our bags together. How long will you stay? Oh, Maud, why don't you just join us?"

"I'll stay until Monday. I guess I feel ready to work

again, and I'm scheduled for every day next week. I'm not giving up on the center, not until they close the doors and lock us out."

"In January? And then you could stay until you start school in the fall. That is, if you still want to start school. Will you?"

She had no answer for him. It would come in time, but not tonight. He waited, hoping. Maud didn't speak. Instead, she moved and lay alongside him, where she could take comfort in his company and look for guidance in the stars.

· Part IV ·

Come In from the Cold

Married at nineteen.

When I called Gumbo in Toronto last night and told him I'd just gotten married he asked, Have you started doing drugs, man?

When I called Mom and told her the news, she asked, Isn't that a little too traditional for a hippie commune?

It's a sign of commitment, I explained.

Sure as hell is, and I'm glad you realize that much, she said.

I was glad she wasn't mad that we hadn't invited her. Maud's dad was in Ireland, I told her.

Can't have one without the other, she agreed. Besides, she said, she knew what it was like to marry in a hustle, to want to do it and do it *now*.

We exchanged a few more words, and I sent my love to Paul. I figured in a few days I'd receive one of her long, breezy, Oh-let-me-tell-you-about letters. But this afternoon while I was working with the building crew, laying concrete for the floor of a second dorm, she arrived. We saw the clouds of dust before we saw any car, and we stopped working while we looked to see who was coming.

A purple Pontiac barreled down the gravel road, and I said, "Oh my gosh, I think it's my mother."

When the car pulled over, one of the guys asked, "Well, Jeffrey, is it?"

I watched her step out of the car. She was wearing a man's shirt, tight red pants, large sunglasses, and high heels. She was blond.

"Yes, it is," I said. "That's my mother."

There were twelve of us working on the building, and she scanned the faces until she spotted me. "Oh, honey," she called, "give me a kiss!"

After I obliged, she gave a general greeting to the others. She fanned herself. "August in Minnesota can be a bitch," she said. "I don't suppose you have something cold to drink." She pushed her sunglasses up and squinted. "Something with a kick?"

One of the women brought her a cup of ginger-spiced water we keep in a barrel near the work site. Mom chugged it down. "Good enough," she said. "Now, Jeff, which one is she?"

"Maud is working with the food crew. I'll take you to meet her." I introduced Mom to the people with me, and she teetered around on her heels and shook hands. One of the women, Carolyn, wouldn't shake, explaining that she'd been up to her elbows in wet concrete and was just too grimy.

"Hell, honey, I work in a slaughterhouse," Mom said as she grabbed and shook. Carolyn's eyes widened, and I saw her suck in a smile.

I grabbed Mom's arm. "Let's go find Maud."

Maud was alone in the kitchen, cleaning fresh-picked vegetables. "Guess who's here?" I called as we stepped in. "This is —"

My mother ran forward, high heels tip-tapping on the concrete floor. She spun Maud around and hugged her.

Maud peered around the blond head and raised an eyebrow. "Your mother?"

Mom stepped back, but she held on to Maud's arms. "Listen, honey, I hope you understand that this boy will never leave you. If you had talked to me first, I would have warned you about that. He's serious, Maud. Now, Tommy was different. Oh, let me tell you about . . ."

We'd hear it all now. I sighed and looked out the window. One of the commune's vans was heading out. Carolyn was driving.

Maud interrupted Mom. "I want to hear everything, but in a short time there will be a roomful of people expecting supper." She gave us each a bowl of peas. "Would you mind shucking these?"

I sat and shucked and listened as the two of them talked and knit their lives together. Because I was concentrating on the stories Maud was telling Mom, stuff she'd never told me, I didn't see the van return or hear anyone approaching.

Carolyn entered, with the others following close behind. She was carrying a case of beer. She set it down, then pulled out a bottle and handed it to my mother. "You wanted something with a kick. We don't usually have any alcohol, but since you are the very first parent to come visit, it seemed like we should celebrate."

"You thought right. And I'll be happy to lift a cold one with all of you. Oh, but not you, honey," she said to Carolyn. "Ginger water for you. Beer isn't good stuff for a pregnant woman. I've put away a lot of booze in my day, but never when I was carrying the boys. Not a drop."

"Will you stay for a while?" someone asked.

Mom shook her head. "And get roped into pouring concrete or milking cows? Not likely, hon."

Mom stayed for supper. By then most of the women were calling each other honey. But not in a mean way. As soon as we finished eating, Mom said good-bye to everyone. She insisted on kisses. Then Maud and I escorted her back to her car, where she hugged us both. She reached up and cupped my face with her long-nailed hands. "This is fine, Jeff. Maud is perfect, and this place is fine. You can leave it all, living here. Just forget all those things that troubled you."

"I'm not here to escape, Mom. None of us is. We're here to build something. Build something better."

She kissed me. "It's fine for that, too. Oh, kids, I gotta go before I start remembering things I don't want to remember and I start crying."

She didn't quite make it. Maud and I waved until the car was out of sight, then looked at each other and we both laughed. We were crying, too.

Maud calls it "Out There." Out there where the wars rage on, the government lies, and every summer another city goes up in flames.

Maud has a group of moles under her right shoulder

218

blade. Seven of them, patterned exactly like Ursa Minor.

Tonight we voted on plans for the next three buildings. We agreed to sell the garden surplus at a roadside stand. Carolyn talked about how much the baby is moving. When her husband lifted her shirt to show the rolling abdomen, it seemed as if the cheering would never end.

If I tap Maud's shoulder with a single finger, she twitches in her sleep. But if I press gently with my whole hand she doesn't move. I like her hair when it's out of the braid and spread loose against her back. A dark shadow against such pale skin.

Mom brought me today's newspaper, and I read it while waiting for Maud to come to bed. Out there, they are still bombing Vietnam. More villages destroyed and won.

We will build more buildings and welcome more members. Three people have left, but two others have joined this past month. There are twenty-five here now. Each member speaks, each is heard. We will expand the garden. The berry bushes will be producing well next summer, enough for us, with more to sell. And after the first child is born here, there will be others. Our turn will come. Someday there will be enough children for a school; we agree we want to teach them here.

Thank God Maud doesn't snore.

We have such wonderful plans.